The Splendid Secrets of 66 Lilly Pilly Lane

Text and cover art copyright © Elena Paige, 2019

The right of Elena Paige to be identified as the author of this work has been asserted by her.

Cover illustration by Andrew Gaia

Cover design by Deranged Doctor Design

Published by Angelos Publishing

Paperback ISBN: 978-1-925557-78-7
Hardback ISBN: 978-1-925557-79-4
Ebook ISBN: 978-1-925557-77-0
Audio Book ISBN: 978-1-925557-81-7

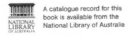

A catalogue record for this book is available from the National Library of Australia

I dedicate this book to Betty Brock for writing
"No Flying in the House."
I read that book when I was in school and have wanted to be
a fairy ever since.

REVIEWS

5 Stars from Readers' Favorite...

"The plot has magic, fantasy, adventure, intrigue, and suspense and Elena Paige knits them together seamlessly, giving the story a good pace and fluidity. There is not one boring moment in the book as readers join Chia in an adventure of fantasy as she tries to break the curse put on her family!"

Mamta Madhavan

"The Splendid Secrets of 66 Lilly Pilly Lane by Elena Paige is a delightful read that includes a powerful lesson. Chia goes through a transformation in the book where she learns self-love and the beauty of the house becomes evident."

Edith Wairimu

The Splendid Secrets of 66 Lilly Pilly Lane

Elena Paige

MS. ROBERTA

Tiredness slid its way up Chia's spine. Dirt furrowed up her fingernails. Cold wrapped itself around her body like fog hunting for a place to settle. She rearranged her head, trying to get comfortable. Oh, but how hard the ground was. How was she ever to feel good sleeping on this cold ground inside these dirty mines?

She hated this place. The horrid, rotten, suffocating mines. They were filled with filth and cold and darkness. She didn't mind the darkness. That was at least familiar. She had lost her sight when she was two years old, and had no memories of seeing. No memories of the sun, the moon, the mines, or the diamonds she was made to dig for every day.

Chia shook off the dirt from her hair. She imagined she was shaking out long and well-washed hair like her twin sister Viola's, rather than her own short, dirty hair. How she missed Viola. How she longed for her voice.

But at least she had her duck for company. Pip was her

constant comfort. Where was Pip? Why couldn't she hear him quacking? He was a noisy duck, thundering about at all hours of the day and night. Chia knew it was because he didn't like the mines. Ducks needed water and light, not darkness and dirt.

"Pip. Where are you?" She reached out both her hands, feeling her way around. She stood up, crossed her arms over her chest, and shivered with worry. "Pip, where have you wandered off to? It's not safe. Pip!" Her chest heaved faster and faster, in and out, as she bent down to feel for some clues.

She often imagined in her mind's eye what her feathered friend must look like. She knew his smell well, just like the old furniture inside the house she used to live in, friendly and familiar. And his soft and cuddly body reminded her of her father. But she didn't know what he looked like. She had never seen a duck. Oh, how she longed to see just for a few minutes. To know what color, and feathers, and even mines looked like.

"You causin' trouble again?"

Chia held her breath at the sound of the voice. Hitchens. The mine master. And the most horrible, unkind, smelly man she had ever met. She hadn't met many men, but she was sure he must be the worst. She couldn't imagine even his own mother liking him.

She took a shallow breath, slumped her shoulders, and leaned her head down toward the ground. "I'm looking for my duck, please, sir. Have you seen him?"

"Don't go acting all prissy with me. I don't care if you're Viola's sister. You work for me down 'ere, and I

won't be treating ya like you're some hoity-toity somethin'
better than me."

SLAP!

Chia felt a sharp pain as Hitchens's hand connected
with her cheek. She was used to the pain, but never the
surprise. She stood her ground and swallowed hard,
crossing her arms against her cold chest. She opened her
eyes as wide as she could and lifted her head, imagining
herself looking into his eyes, which she was convinced
must be as black as his heart.

"Viola would never let you treat me this way!"

SLAP!

"She's the one that told me to slap ya!"

This time Chia fell to the ground, the pain searing
through her fine cheekbone and into her soul. But her
resolve was strong. "Don't slap me. I'm Viola's sister. She
will have your head for this."

Chia couldn't understand what was wrong with her
today. She never, ever dared to speak up to Hitchens. Not
ever.

Hitchens snarled like a wild dog. "I can do anythin' I
darn well please. Ya still harpin' on about ya sister? Viola's
the one who sent ya 'ere. She despises ya. She told me to
work ya to the bone. I'm just followin' her orders!"

Chia was sure her heart skipped a beat from his cruel
words. But she refused to listen. Refused to believe. Viola
loved her. She would never do such a thing. Hitchens was
taunting her with his lies. It was Priscilla, their stepmother,
who had done this. It had to be. Viola was sure to come
and save her any day now.

Chia gritted her teeth as Hitchens continued to yell and hiss at her. She didn't plan to lash out and be punished again. But her mouth had a mind of its own. "Be quiet, you horrid man. You're the most disgusting person I've ever met. Viola will make you suffer for this."

SLAP!

Chia waited for the pain to arrive. Instead, a strange bubbling sensation spread from the spot where Hitchens' hand touched her on the cheek. An electric sensation sprung up her face, through her eyes, to the back of her head, and down her spine. She felt strong and brave and protected somehow.

"Viola hates ya! Ya got that? Did I make it simple for ya?"

His laughter echoed off the mine walls, making Chia feel like crying. But she didn't. She couldn't. Pip needed her. She had to find him. She shook the magical feeling away and focused on her pet duck. "I need to find—"

"Don't ya dare mention that duck. Miss Priscilla decided ya duck would be a fine dinner." He spat something juicy and gulped hard. "I took care of 'im."

Hitchens's words scratched through Chia's ears and nestled into the pit of her stomach. The stale piece of bread Chia ate for breakfast crept its way back up her throat. She gagged. She didn't know what she would do if something had happened to her duck. Not Pip!

She didn't care what happened to her. But Pip was her only friend. Kneeling down, she bowed to her captor. "Please, please, he makes me work harder. Please! He's all the light I have."

"Don't ya go makin' me pity ya 'cause ya blind. I don't care if that duck is ya sun. He's a dead duck now. Too late!"

Chia cradled her head and listened to Hitchens' footsteps crumble the ground as he stomped away. She wanted to run after him and demand he do as she ask. She was the lady of the house. Or had been, alongside her sister, before *she* had arrived. Before her father had married Priscilla.

Before she was sent here to work hard finding *her* diamonds. Making *her* rich.

Chia refused to believe Pip was dead. She could feel it in the pit of her stomach. He was alive. She had to believe he was. He was all she had, next to Viola. But she couldn't walk around the mines on her own. It was too dangerous without Pip guiding her with his quacks. She sank deeper into the dirt and the darkness, wondering how she would ever find her duck. The duck her father had gifted her right before he died. Right before Priscilla took her father from her forever. Pip and Viola were all she had. She had to rescue them. To get them far away from the mines and from Priscilla.

"Is that horrible man gone? Goodness me, he's awfully smelly, and so rude. How do you put up with him?"

Chia sat up, startled by the strange voice. She held her breath as the words floated through the air as if spoken by her guardian angel. Someone else was in the mines. Someone other than herself, Pip, or Hitchens.

Chia lifted her head toward the sound of the vanilla voice. Her heart beat so fast, she couldn't find any words to reply. But she felt safe and protected. Something about the voice made her trust it. It was light and pure and sparkled.

"Come along. You don't want to sit around in this dark and dank place all day, do you? The house is waiting for you."

Chia closed her eyes and surrendered to the woman's words. Was she about to be rescued? Warmth crawled up her back and around her neck for the first time in a long time.

"The house? Who . . . are . . . you?"

"How rude of me not to introduce myself. I'm Ms. Roberta. I've come to take you back to where you really belong."

"I belong with my sister."

"You want to leave the mines, don't you?"

Chia could think of nothing nicer than leaving the mines. But she couldn't leave her sister behind and tromp away with some stranger, no matter how sweet her voice was. "How did you find me here? How did you get in? Hitchens blocks the entrance. Did you see a duck by any chance?"

"Yes, your duck. Don't worry one bit about Pip. I've already whisked him away to 66 Lilly Pilly Lane. He's waiting there for you."

A fluttery feeling Chia had never experienced before moved through her stomach and into her chest. "Where is that?" Her head wanted nothing more than to go anywhere with this mysterious woman. But her feet trembled with fear. What if Hitchens caught her? "You've definitely rescued Pip? He's safe?"

"Yes, child. Don't listen to that bully. He didn't lay a finger on Pip, I promise. He's fine. And more than likely feasting on worms while waiting for you. Now put this on. You look a mess in that outfit. And it's most unflattering."

Chia reached out both her hands in the voice's direction. She felt material, soft and silky, and wondered if she really ought to put something this fine on.

"I know you can't see it, but oh, what a beautiful dress it is. One of Viola's finest. It was laid out for her to wear to the ball tomorrow. But I dare say she doesn't deserve it."

Chia stiffened. "This is Viola's dress? I can't wear it. Please send it back to her."

"I will not. She deserves nothing after what she's done to you."

"Please, miss. Viola is good. I promise. If this is her dress, she'll be most upset it was taken. I couldn't possibly wear it. Please return it to her."

Silence filled the air as if Ms. Roberta was weighing up Chia's request.

"No. I think it most definitely belongs to you. Now put it on, child, before the mine master returns. You don't want to miss your chance of escape, do you?"

Chia turned her back to the voice, her hands trembling. Her mind was saying no, but she had already pulled off her potato-sack top and pulled on the dress. It was light and fluttery, like she was wearing air. She pulled off her pants, glad to be rid of them, and threw them onto the ground. "What color is the dress?"

"It's white. As white as snow. It suits you. I know these

shoes don't really match, but it's important you wear them."

Chia reached her hands out again, wondering what shoes she would be given. Her face lit up as she felt the rubber. "Rain boots! My favorite." They reminded her of the days she spent stomping through puddles with her father.

"Red ones, in case you're wondering. Now take my hand, and let's get out of this nasty place. I need fresh air in a hurry."

Chia didn't know what red or white looked like, but she imagined they were marvelous. She reached out her hand, expecting a hand as soft as Ms. Roberta's voice to take her own, but she felt something cold and hard. Like steel. Or metal.

"Is that your hand?" she said, pulling away as if she had touched a bomb about to explode. "What are you?"

"I'm terribly sorry I shocked you. I forget what I am sometimes. I'll explain everything once we're out of here. Now take my hand, and don't worry about it being so cold. Cold hands means faster travel!"

Chia tried to push away her curiosity, but she desperately wanted to know what Ms. Roberta was. She imagined a half robot, half human. Or perhaps a pirate queen with a hook for a hand. But as the five fingers touched her own again, her curiosity spun away, a blurred buzzing filling her head instead. Spinning erupted in her brain. It was as if she were falling down a rabbit hole, deeper and deeper, faster and faster. Could she possibly be asleep and dreaming this all up? She squeezed tightly the hand in hers and wished with all her might that this might truly be real. That she may finally have some happiness. A tiny morsel of joy. A glimmer of hope. That perhaps for the first time in her entire twelve years of life, something good might finally happen.

Finally.

But her mind flashed images of Viola and Priscilla and Hitchens. They would fly into a wild rage when they discovered her gone. Viola would feel betrayed and left behind. And who would find Priscilla's diamonds for her? She stilled her spinning mind and yelled out, "Wait. I have to go back!"

But deep down she knew, it was too late.

2

66 LILLY PILLY LANE

Chia's chest felt like a boulder had successfully crushed her lungs. After yelling that she needed to go back, she felt like she'd been sucked through a straw and swallowed. She opened her mouth like a puffer fish and gobbled in the fresh country air. Fresh country air? Her nose picked up scents of the salty ocean breeze. Where was she?

She wasn't in the mines anymore, of this she was sure. She breathed in deeply, filling her lungs with more air, and yelled, "I need to go back!"

"Oh, no need for that. You'll love it here. You really will."

"Viola. Diamonds. I have to . . . Take me back!" Chia had never felt worse about anything she'd ever done. She was a monster. Selfish beyond words. She was mad at herself for considering it, even for a moment.

Ms. Roberta's cold hard hand squeezed Chia's more tightly. "I can't take you back, I'm afraid. It will be fine, you'll see. All the help you need is inside. I promise we'll help you, Chia. Now you'd best go in. The house is waiting for you."

Chia's chest heaved with a mixture of frustration and exhilaration. The house was waiting for her? Her head was still spinning violently, like a tornado had worked its way up through her stomach and settled into her brain.

"Quack quack!"

"Pip! Pip, is that you? Is it really you, Pip?" Chia dropped Ms. Roberta's hand and stood up, almost falling backward again. She used the bounce of her red rain boots to propel her forward. Bending over, she felt around for her beloved duck. Her one true friend. Pip.

Chia moved aside the barrage of flowers at her feet. Lots and lots of flowers growing wild all around her. She breathed in the sweet scents and allowed herself to smile as she felt the warmth of duck feathers. "Pip, I'm so glad you're alive and that horrible Hitchens didn't hurt you."

She scooped the duck up into her arms and hugged him more tightly than a teddy. Pip snuggled his head in her armpit, relaxing in her arms like he always did, quacking happily.

"Oh, what a sweet reunion. Anyway, I must dash. I promised Robert I'd visit, and I mustn't be late. But I will see you later."

Chia couldn't believe it. Ms. Roberta had bought her to this strange new place and was about to leave her by herself. "Please don't leave me here alone. I don't know what I'm supposed to do."

"Just climb the steps in front of you and ring the door knocker. And do ask Heidi to give you a bath."

"But I'm blind!"

"Yes, dear, I know. But you'll work it out. You'll be fine."

"Please don't go. I'm scared." Chia's bottom lip trembled.

"I believe in you, Chia. I will be back later, I promise. Don't worry, Artemis will take care of you. Welcome to 66 Lilly Pilly Lane. Goodbye. Goodbye!"

"Wait! Who's Artemis? Come back!"

But firm footsteps marched away like they belonged to a dinosaur rather than a petite woman. Chia imagined Ms. Roberta must be light and dainty and oh so pretty. She imagined her to be wearing lace and silk and feathers. Chia remembered her own pretty dress. Viola's dress, which had been stolen.

She relaxed her shoulders and her guilt for a moment and allowed herself to feel the soft texture in her hands and to breathe in the material's freshness. She had never worn something so light and luxurious in all of her life. Even when her father had been alive, she had always worn practical clothes. *Money doesn't define you, Chia. Kindness does. And you don't need to wear things that make you look down on others,* he would say.

Viola hated his view on fashion, and after his death, the first thing she did was throw away all her practical clothes and replace them with the finest fabrics and most fashionable styles.

"Quack quack!"

"Yes, Pip, you're absolutely right. We can't stand out here all day." She was blind, but her other senses more than made up for it. She tuned into the surrounding space, pushing aside her questions of how she had arrived. Ms. Roberta had said she was at 66 Lilly Pilly Lane.

She turned around slowly, judging her new surroundings. She couldn't feel the sun on her skin, which meant there were more houses on this street. But it was so quiet. No movement, no people, no cars on the road, no horses roaming in the countryside. Was everyone still asleep? Chia felt tired, hungry, frightened, and excited all at once. The mystery all around her beckoned. Perhaps, something good was about to happen. Perhaps, things might finally go right. Perhaps, she might find the help she needed here, to save Viola from her nasty stepmother, Priscilla.

"Quack, quack, quaaaack," said Pip, pulling his head out from under her arm and wriggling to be set free.

Chia held onto him tightly. "So you think we should run away? Not go into the house? Really?" Chia pretended to understand him. She felt forward with her feet, finding the first step. "One, two, three," she counted.

She meandered all the way up to number nine. Nine steps to the front door. She placed Pip down on the ground and scrunched her face as she heard him scamper back down the stairs toward the weeds and the wild flowers that surrounded the house.

"Coward. Come back. We have to go in. I mean, what's the worst that can happen?" She coughed out her fear, breathed in hope, braced her shoulders, and turned back toward the door. Pip had scampered away. "Something magical brought us here. Maybe magic is real.

Maybe someone here can help me save Viola. I have to try anything, Pip. Please understand. Please come with me?"

"*Quack, quack, quack,*" came the sound from beside her.

Chia smiled, relieved her duck had returned to her side. "You are a good friend. I won't forget this, Pip."

She imagined the house before her. Perhaps a cream-colored building with a big black door. Her heart thumped like a wild horse on the run. She breathed in the perfumed smells of the land all around her. The birds twittered as they searched for their morning meal. The cold wind urged her to escape into warmth.

She reached out and touched the door knocker. It was shaped like a teardrop and made of heavy cast iron. She lifted it up, but placed it down softly again, hesitating. What color was it? Perhaps green like the grass. She didn't know what green looked like. She wondered if a memory of it lingered somewhere in her mind.

After all, she had been able to see until the fever took her sight away when she was two years old. She imagined green to feel warm and comforting, like a soft bed cover. She imagined the color green to fill her up like freshly baked bread, butter, honey, and love.

Chia moved her hands to the left and felt numbers. Red numbers, she decided. Sixty-six, three-dimensional, and alive to her touch. Tingles of electricity weaved their way up her spine. All she had to do was tap the door knocker and all her troubles might be resolved.

Instead, nervous and tense, she pulled up her socks, nestled inside her rain boots, and tugged at her dress with her hand. What if they turned her away? What if Ms. Roberta had tricked her? She hadn't stayed, after all.

"We'll sleep here and wait until morning," she said, knowing full well it already was morning.

She lay down on the cold concrete atop the stairs and leaned on the door for some warmth. Her faithful duck cuddled up beside her. She closed her eyes and pushed away the worries and fears crowded inside her head. What was this house that Ms.Roberta kept referring to as if it were a person?

She didn't know if she'd be let in, and she didn't want to find out just yet. She had been disappointed so many times before. She wasn't ready for more disappointment today. Not yet.

Creak! Crackle! Bang!

Chia swept Pip up in her arms and jumped to her feet, almost falling backward down the stairs she had so carefully climbed.

She held her breath. Who had opened the door? She waited patiently for someone to invite her inside. But no one did. She reached out her hands. The door was open. Should she walk through? She was so nervous and excited all at the same time she felt like she might burst into a million rainbow-colored balloons.

She closed her eyes tight and decided it might be worth stepping through the door into 66 Lilly Pilly Lane. Who or what would she find inside?

3

JEREMY

Chia trembled from her feet to the tips of her frazzled hair. Why was she hesitating? She turned back toward the steps and considered jumping all nine in one leap and running all the way back home. Back home to her sister. Back home to Priscilla, the nasty stepmother who had married her father, driven him to his grave, treated Viola like she was a princess, and treated Chia like she was a slave.

But she didn't know the way home.

And the glimmer of hope that lit up in her chest moved up into her eyes. She could see hope for once. A way to help Viola.

She jutted her chin forward, turned back toward the door, and dared herself to enter. Her only choice was to walk through the door.

"Well, are you going to stand there all day, or are you going to come in? I hope that duck is for my dinner."

Startled, Chia stood up straight. The voice was severe and pompous, like it belonged to a king. She noticed the voice seemed to float up to her from foot level. Perhaps it was a dwarf, she decided. Nothing seemed impossible given the way she had traveled here.

"Are you daydreaming? Come in. I'm hungry, and duck is my *favorite* meal."

Chia frowned and turned one shoulder away from the direction of the voice. She reached out for Pip and found him beside her left leg, shaking as if he completely understood every word being said about him. She swept him up, her temper trembling. "Pip is not for dinner. He's my friend, and if that's what happens to poor innocent animals around here, then I'm not staying." She took two defiant steps backward, feeling her socks sink into her boots again.

"How can anyone not adore delicious duck? I could eat duck all day long. Fried, roasted, poached, and toasted. Why, I can even eat it raw if I have to. You're not a vegetarian, are you? I detest vegetarians."

"I'm sorry if I offend you. But I don't eat meat. It's cruel, mean, and unkind to hurt other living beings." Chia took another angry step backwards. Avoiding falling down the steps she dropped Pip. He quacked and quivered about as if he knew the discussion was about him being made into dinner.

"It's alright, Pip, I won't let this horrid hungry boy with no manners eat you. I won't!" She pulled up her socks and stood up again, stomping her red rain boots in disgust. She stepped forward a few paces cautiously. She couldn't see her surroundings, and her temper had dulled her other senses.

"Who are you calling a boy? Are you blind *and* stupid?" said the voice, testing her patience.

Chia wanted to jump forward and cover his mouth so he would stop speaking. But she didn't. Instead, she remembered to keep her manners in check. She was here for Viola, not for herself. She bit her tongue and pressed her lips together tight so as not to say something she would regret. She didn't want to be turned away, after all.

"Jeremy, stop teasing our guests." A new voice spoke. It was commanding yet sincere. "Come in. Come in. Don't mind this little fellow."

Chia felt warmth and kindness rush over her like the sun on an autumn day. This voice was smooth, sensitive, deep, and dreamy. Not at all like the rude boy's voice. She imagined it belonged to a round, rustic man, dressed in loose white pants with a matching top, who had a long white beard that would make any wizard jaded and jealous. But she still felt cross with the boy who threatened to eat her duck.

"I demand you leave my duck alone and return him at once!" As the words left her mouth, she felt the soft down of duck feathers against her cheek. Someone had picked Pip up and was handing him to her. She reached her hands out to take him, relaxing her shoulders and her anger. "Thank you."

"Come in. Please come in. Jeremy and I don't bite. I promise," chuckled the kind voice. "I'm assuming you came to see Clariel?"

Chia felt a little faint, and her muscles quivered. "I don't know why I'm here. A lady brought me."

"Ah yes," said the deep comforting voice. "You're Chia. Ms. Roberta brought you. Come in, come in, we were expecting you, weren't we, Jeremy?"

Chia felt all resistance leave her body. Her bones hurt for a warm bath, her stomach cried for food, and her muscles ached for human company. She had felt so alone in the mines apart from her pet duck. Pip was a constant comfort, but he didn't talk back to her, so she always felt like she was talking to herself.

"I never agreed to this. I think it's still a rotten idea to bring her here, and even meaner to tease me with that delicious, tantalizing duck. Have you ever tasted duck souffle?" Jeremy complained.

"Quack, quack, QUACK!" Pip nestled his head in Chia's armpit, shaking at Jeremy's suggestion.

"Why, you horrid boy!" Chia wanted to kick out in all directions. To kick Jeremy away. That would teach him to say such nasty things. After all she'd gone through, after all her torment. But she didn't. She held her temper.

"What's the matter, no fight in you?" laughed Jeremy, his voice full of snark.

Chia detested him more than Hitchens, and she hadn't thought it was possible to hate anyone more than him.

Jeremy continued his rant. "I doubt Clariel wants to see this girl. She's as mighty as a mouse. I think the house made a mistake letting her in!"

Chia started to breathe heavily. She wanted to yell at this prickly, pious, pushy boy. To make him see that the house didn't make a mistake. She concentrated on the kind and gentle *tut tut* the kind voice was making to hush the loud-mouthed Jeremy from saying anything more.

"Don't mind Jeremy. He's protective of the house. He means no harm. My name is Artemis."

He didn't seem as annoyed with Jeremy as she was feeling.

"Nice to meet you." Chia let herself relax slightly, and she calmed her tidal wave of temper at the sound of Artemis's reassurance. His soft and gentle chuckle reminded her of her father. How she missed being swung in the air by his strong arms. He would pretend to drop her, only to catch her on the way down. Then they would both fall softly and roll and roll on the soft grass of Lavender Hill, where her beautiful cottage was. How she longed to be there now.

Chia swallowed abruptly as something hard touched the palm of her left hand. It was dry and brittle. Like wood. Her hand tightened around it.

"Come, I've many things to show you," said Artemis, his voice closer. Was this his walking stick? His wand? First, Ms. Roberta's cold, hard hand, now this. What was this magic? Who were these people, really?

She nodded and let her boots carry her forward one small, unsure step at a time, her hand wrapped tightly around the wood. From the way the sound was drifting away without echo, she imagined she was standing in a giant white room.

"Artemis, I implore you to reconsider having this dirty girl in 66 Lilly Pilly Lane. We can do this without her.

And I think it's cruel to bring a duck in here and taunt me like this."

Artemis chuckled, but his voice sounded more severe. "Jeremy, settle down. The decision is made. Now off you go and fetch Heidi. Chia needs a bath. And so does the duck, which will not be for your supper today. Or ever."

Chia listened as Jeremy huffed and puffed. She wasn't sure if he left the room or not. She heard no footsteps. Chia lifted her head and dropped more of her tension. She hoped Jeremy was finally gone. Pip relaxed in her arms. She longed for nothing more than a nice hot bath. And clean clothes and a sumptuous, soft bed. But she needed to know where she was and why she was here. Most importantly, she needed to find out if these people could and would help her save her sister. Her sister was all that mattered to her.

"Mr. Artemis, sir, why am I here? And how did I get here? It all happened so quickly, and I was spinning, and then suddenly, well, I mean to say, I wonder if I'm dreaming—and you are a wonderful dream—but I need to wake up now. I have to save my sister. And who is Clariel?" Chia ran out of breath, or she would have continued asking questions. It wasn't exactly what she had planned to say, but she had a terrible habit of wanting to say one thing and then saying something entirely different.

"Never mind that, child. I will explain what you need to know, but first things first. You shall have sight!"

Chia didn't understand what Artemis meant, but music played as if on cue. It was grand, heroic music and reminded her instantly of her father playing piano. Oh, how she loved the feeling of the melody dancing in her ears.

An unexpected burst of energy accompanied the music and pushed through her eyes, like electricity being generated, or the sun bursting inside her eyeballs. She couldn't control her racing heart, which beat like she had run down the steepest hill. Her tummy fluttered as if she was turned upside down and right way up again very quickly. She fell backward on what felt like soft moss and covered her mouth with both her hands. She spread her eyes wide open.

She could see.

Oh my, could she see!

And what she saw was nothing like what she had imagined.

She could see, and the sight was so splendid, so spectacular, so sensational, so satisfying, she did what any girl who saw light and color and shapes and forms for the first time since she was a toddler would do. She dropped Pip, scrunched her eyes tightly shut, plunged herself back into darkness, turned toward the door, and ran out of the house as fast as her red rain boots would carry her.

4

ARTEMIS

Chia didn't bother opening her eyes. Instead, she held her breath and counted away her feelings. A habit she had picked up as a child. She held her breath when she felt anxious, worried, scared. Which was most of the time. She was only ever treated badly, and she never expected good things to happen these days. She held her breath and counted *one . . . two . . . three*. She counted away her fear. Her shock. Her disbelief. She needed to leave this house. She had not asked for her sight, and it scared her, confused her, overwhelmed her, and delighted her. But the house and Artemis and, and, and . . . so many things she didn't expect and didn't understand.

She ran down the stairs, not counting them properly, her eyes still shut tight. She tripped and flew through the air, landing on her bottom at the base of the stairs, her dress ripped, her skin torn, and her mind racing.

Holding her breath wasn't working one bit today.

What should she do? Stay or go? Her brain was

bursting with light and color and craving more. Her mind could think only of fear. Fear of failing Viola.

"Come back, Chia. Please come back."

Artemis was calling her. Kindness and concern in his voice. She tightened her eyes a little more. Something hard and strong wound its way around her waist. It was too fast for her to resist, and she hadn't the physical strength to fight it. "I need to go home. I don't belong here. All this magic, and I'm blind. I need to be blind." She felt herself lifted high off the ground. "Put me down. Please put me down."

She opened her eyes, curiosity and fear meeting each other like old friends. She screamed, her voice as shrill and chilling as a barn owl. She hadn't expected to scream. She didn't scream because of being lifted off the ground. She didn't scream because it was Artemis who had lifted her.

She screamed because Artemis was a tree! A tall, woody, alive tree. One of his many long brittle branches was curled around her waist.

"I will bring you back inside the house. I'm very sorry I didn't warn you before giving you your sight back," said Artemis.

Chia, still tense, her mind racing for answers, allowed Artemis to carry her inside. As the breeze from the outdoors shifted to the warmth of inside, and the doors closed behind her, she breathed out in delight at the sights all around her. She couldn't not. Despite all that was happening, this room was bursting to be looked at and enjoyed.

"I am terribly sorry I didn't warn you I was a tree. It's

not something one can explain with ease and grace. It was most insensitive of me." Artemis gently laid Chia down.

Chia opened her eyes as wide as a child at Christmas time and willed herself to stop spinning. Her feet wanted to turn back toward the door and run again, but she coaxed them to stay. Her heart seemed to skip several beats as her eyes hungrily sucked in the spectacle all around her.

Before her stood Artemis. Who was indeed a tree. He towered above her much higher than his voice had originally revealed, gentle and giant and grand. His trunk, a pale brown color, shook with layers of paper bark, which hung like ornaments from a Christmas tree. His chiseled face peeked out from the center of his tall trunk—a nose, a mouth, and two bright coloured eyes. They glimmered with laughter and light and shone like twinkling stars.

"What color are your eyes?" she asked.

"As blue as the sky."

Chia followed the trunk upward as it stretched so high she couldn't see the top. Countless branches reached out so far she wondered how they fit inside the house. A mixture of different shaded leaves danced upon the branches, with posies dropping petals as if a soft breeze were coaxing them free.

"I've surprised you. Are you not pleased to have your sight back?" Artemis spoke softly. Almost a whisper.

Chia blinked several times. She couldn't stop blinking. She wanted to speak, but her eyes locked into Artemis's blue ones and settled there. Her brain felt twisted and knotted up like the branches of the tree that stood before her.

"There is magic in this house. Magic you have yet to understand. I will explain it all to you in time, but please, first let yourself enjoy the marvels." He motioned with his long branches at the room all around them.

Oh, what a room!

Chia indulged her senses, especially her sight, which was starved of light and color and movement. She could see! And the splendor before her made up for all her years of darkness. The wonder and magic of it all fluttered through her whole body, making her feel light-headed. It was beyond anything she could have made up in her own imagination.

She was standing inside a room that stretched on and on all around her and above her, as if it were a world of its own. The ceiling, or where the ceiling ought to have been, shimmered with sparkling water. Chia was sure she was seeing things. Imagining as she always did to escape her reality. If this was a dream, she was impressed with her level of creativity. She held her breath as she spotted an upside down waterfall splashing into the water ceiling, forming bubbles in the water and in her stomach.

How was this possible?

"You haven't seen everything. Go on, let yourself explore." Artemis's voice was encouraging and filled her with strength and courage.

Chia had never met anyone so kind. She threw herself on the tree, her arms hardly reaching halfway around the thickly set trunk. "Thank you."

"Here, let me help you get a better view," he replied,

his branches gently entwining Chia around the waist again.

"I'm sorry if I'm heavy."

"Nonsense. You are far too light. I will give you food and a bath, I promise, but first . . . ah, see the sights before you."

As she lifted off the ground a second time, Chia allowed herself to enjoy it this time. She felt like a butterfly and spread out her arms as if flying. She surrendered to the giddy feeling in her stomach and the shivers running up and down her spine. Below her was the most marvelous room she had ever seen. It was bigger than many ballrooms joined together. The ground was dotted with moss so soft it looked like soft pillows of marshmallows. And so green and lush and velvety. She longed to be back on the ground able to run her fingers through it. To roll and frolic like she did when she was younger and carefree.

Spread across the moss were flowers and toadstools, much bigger than normal, and small teepees painted different colors that looked like they were made from Artemis's bark. Chia didn't know which color was which other than green, but she loved them all. And she had been right; not only did green feel like freshly baked bread with butter and honey, all the colors did.

And there was a tube slide! Chia was sure it must be the longest slide in existence. It weaved its way around the room like a giant boa constrictor and finished on a massive sand pit, where soft buttery sandcastles glowed as though made from crushed diamonds rather than sand.

"What is this place? I'm not . . . in Heaven, am I?"

"It is all as real as you and me, right here on planet Earth. You're alive, and no, you're definitely not dreaming," said Artemis, lifting her higher.

Chia reached out her hands, daring to touch the water ceiling. The cool wet of the water calmed her aching heart and racing mind. It was real water.

"What are those?" Chia pointed in awe at large pieces of paper cut into triangles floating all around her. They had string tails covered in ribbons. She felt transfixed by their beauty and soft gentle movements despite there being no wind in the room.

"They are kites. Have you never flown one?"

"No, I haven't." Chia began to understand how much she had missed out on.

"You will. All in good time. But where are my manners? You must be famished. Yes, of course, you're hungry. Let's get you some food before Jeremy returns with Heidi."

Artemis floated Chia gently back to the ground.

Chia pushed her delight and pleasure away, stomping her foot on the soft moss, mad at herself. She shouldn't be enjoying herself. She should be helping her Viola. "Pip. Where are you? I've lost Pip. What a bad, bad person I am."

"Why do you speak this way about yourself? You are a wonderful person."

"No, not at all, sir. I am terrible. Not deserving of this wonderful place. I shouldn't be here. I think Ms. Roberta found the wrong girl. You should return me to the mines. That's where I belong."

"Nonsense. I don't know why you think this way about yourself. You are kind and thoughtful and sweet."

Chia swallowed Artemis's words like they were hard nuts scratching their way down her throat. Her mind returned to her constant thoughts of having abandoned her sister, and how angry Priscilla would be when she discovered her missing from the mines. She closed her eyes, depriving herself of the delights that stood before her.

"Open your eyes, child. Be kind to yourself."

Chia felt a gentle breeze on her face. She peeked one eye open and saw Artemis swaying before her, his face level to her own. "A good person always puts others first. I can't afford to get distracted here. I must save my sister. I don't believe you can help me after all. Please take me back. Please?"

"Nonsense. You must learn to love yourself first. It is yourself that you need to look after, not everyone else."

Chia didn't understand. Put herself first? That would make her selfish and unkind.

Artemis cleared his throat and frowned. "Have you ever asked yourself why your sister hasn't bothered to help you? Are you sure she deserves your help?"

Chia took a step back and crossed her arms. "Yes, of course she does. Oh, Hitchens says terrible things about her. But none of them are true. She would have come to save me, I'm sure of it, as soon as she found some time. She's very busy with all the parties she has to host. She's the lady of the house and all, who could blame her? And oh, her dress." Chia looked down at her dress, covered in blood and dirt. "I've totally ruined it."

Artemis shook his branches from side to side as if disagreeing with her. "Chia, you must put yourself first for a change. You're very special. And Viola needs to take responsibility for her choices and actions."

Chia furrowed her brow. "No, I'm sorry, sir, but I couldn't possibly put myself first. I won't. I can't. Pip? Where has my duck wandered off to? Pip!"

Chia looked around, trying to spot her duck in among the flowers and the birds and the butterflies that suddenly seemed to emerge from thin air. It was delightful. And a good distraction from what Artemis was saying. She closed her eyes tight once more and yelled for her duck to come. "Pip! Come here. Come here, I say!"

"I'm coming, I'm coming. Geez already!"

Chia opened her eyes so fast and wide they almost fell off her face. She looked to the left and then to the right. "Who said that?"

"I did!" Pip waddled toward her, lifting his wing and waving at her.

"You can talk? My ears must be filled with so much wax I'm hearing things. I'm delirious. This house isn't good for me." She fell backward onto a toadstool.

"There ain't no way I'm ever leaving here, Chia. Not ever. If this place is Heaven, then I've never been happier to be dead. It's worth risking being eaten by that nasty fox to stay here," said Pip.

Chia shook her head. The magic and marvel was

making her feel nervous again. She could not only see, but her duck was talking.

"What fox?" she asked.

Artemis swayed from side to side, smiling so broadly his mouth seemed to stretch beyond the limits of his trunk. "You'll feel better about all this once you've had something to eat and a nice warm bath."

Chia tapped her foot, contemplating whether to stay or go. She didn't want to get too comfortable in this strange magical land. She needed to focus on saving Viola and avoid getting distracted at any cost.

"Please, Chia. Can we have a little something to eat? Please?"

Chia looked into Pip's big brown eyes. Her duck was talking to her. And he was so sweet. He drooped his head and looked so sad; she didn't want to let him down.

"Maybe something small. Quickly. Then we either get help to save Viola, or we leave and do it ourselves. Agreed?"

"Yippee!" Pip flew out of her arms and flapped around like he really was being chased by a fox. He turned to Artemis, his bill dripping with drool. "What you got, big fella? I'm starving!"

Artemis waved his branches as if he were a genie about to grant a wish. "I'm pleased to fill your stomach with whatever you can think of. Do me the kind honor of pulling some bark from my trunk, would you, Mr. Pip?"

Pip waddled over to the large tree that towered over him, leaned his bill forward, and grasped a piece of the paper-like bark that hung from Artemis's trunk. He placed it on the ground and looked up at Artemis for further instructions. "I said I was starving, right? I'm not that into bark, though I bet it's tasty for a woodpecker."

Artemis waved his branches more vigorously. "I wouldn't think of disappointing you. Ask the paper for what you want to eat. It's as simple as that."

"Really? Hey, Chia, watch me. I can do magic. I'll have two worm burgers with lettuce as the bread, a side of fries, and a chocolate shake. And a strawberry sundae."

"Pip. That's too much to ask for!" Chia couldn't believe her ears, nor her eyes. The paper bark starting jumping about like it couldn't decide where it wanted to land, then transformed into a small wooden table topped with all the food Pip had asked for. Just like that.

"*Mm.* This food is good. I really was starving. Who eats dried bread? I mean, someone ought to hang Hitchens upside down and shake the cobwebs from him. Everyone knows bread is bad for ducks. *Mm. Mm!* Delicious!"

"Your turn, Chia. Take a piece of bark and ask for what you want," said Artemis.

Chia stroked her chin, not sure what to ask for. She felt guilty, but she was starving. She tried to convince herself this would be fun. Wasn't she allowed some fun? Just a little?

She reached out her hand, marveling at the shades of what she guessed was brown. She carefully peeled a piece of the bark. "Does that hurt you?"

"Not at all. Now ask for what you want. And please do treat yourself. You deserve it."

Chia didn't believe she did. She had to save Viola, and

eating felt unkind and selfish. But her stomach growled from hunger. "A bowl of vegetable soup, if it's not too much to ask for."

The paper bark lay still for several seconds, like it was too hard to make soup. But then it danced its way to life and turned into a little table. A white bowl of steaming hot soup appeared from thin air.

"Is that really all you want? You could have cake and ice cream and candies. And hot bread and—"

"It doesn't matter what I want. This is enough. And more than I deserve." Chia stood at the table, which was just the right height for her, and took a sip of the hot vegetable soup. It glided down her throat, warming up her insides. "It's delicious. Compliments to the chef."

Before she could take another mouthful, she clutched at her chest, dropping her spoon with a splash! A small brightly colored something-or-other creature jumped toward her out of nowhere. Grasping for her spoon, she pointed it toward what looked like a fox. "Stay back or I'll —I'll—"

"Chia, that's—" But Pip didn't get to explain.

"Why, you dirty little girl. I knew I shouldn't have let you in. To think I went to all the trouble for you to see Clariel, and for what? Send her away, Artemis, I insist, and let me keep the duck!"

Pip hid behind his table, a mouthful of worms dripping from his bill. "Stand back, you crazy pink fox! I ain't no one's dinner," said Pip.

"Jeremy? You're Jeremy?" said Chia, now recognizing the voice from earlier and hardly able to believe what was happening. That was what Pip had meant about a fox. Jeremy was a fox. A bright pink fox.

Artemis swayed, leaned down a branch, and embraced the fox, who looked like he was about to pounce on the duck. He lifted him off the ground as he kicked and screamed in protest.

"Let me at him. Just because I'm pink don't mean I can't fight you. Let me down, Artemis. That duck is destined to be my supper." He turned his pointy furred face to Chia. "And you! You have your sight and your talking duck. So leave now, why don't you?"

"Jeremy, that's enough from you," said Artemis. He dropped the little pink fox down the giant winding slide. "My apologies, he's harmless, I assure you."

Chia wasn't convinced. Jeremy hadn't said a single nice thing about her since she'd arrived.

"I will eat your duck when I get out of heeeeere!" Jeremy's voice echoed from inside the tube slide.

"Eat me? Help! Help! I'm in mortal danger." Pip jumped into Chia's arms and flapped about in a frenzy instead of settling.

"It's fine. I won't let him hurt you. I promise," she reassured him.

Pip popped his head back out, looking around in case the fox was free. "Don't put me down. Not ever. Oh my . . . on second thought, let me free. Put me down this instant."

Chia wasn't sure what had suddenly gotten into Pip. He couldn't seem to decide what he wanted.

"Chia, Chia, Chia. Put me down . . . I think. I think. I

think . . . I'm . . . IN LOVE!" said Pip, flapping about madly until Chia released him.

What had gotten into her duck? But then she spotted it. Another duck. A bright-colored duck with the biggest eyes. Chia laughed. She hadn't laughed in so long she wasn't used to the feeling in her belly. It felt good.

"Artemis," announced the new duck. "Clariel would like to see the girl." She blinked her long eyelashes and looked down at the moss, avoiding eye contact with Pip.

"Thank you, Heidi! I think Chia will need a bath and her dress mended before she does that. Chia?" Artemis's voice was almost as soft as a whisper. "Clariel can help you save your sister. She's the reason Ms. Roberta brought you here. She has the answer you seek."

Chia sat on a toadstool, trembling from anticipation. Could whoever Clariel was really help her? Should she trust these strangers? Chia fidgeted with her dress. It was worth the risk, she decided. Anything was worth the risk if it meant saving her sister. "I would rather see her now, please."

"You're not seeing anyone without a bath," said Heidi, marching toward her with determination in her waddle.

"Forget her. Bathe me. Bathe me!" Pip stalked about like a common chicken, flapping his wings and showing off for Heidi.

Heidi's duck cheeks went slightly pale, and she looked away, pretending Pip wasn't making a spectacle of himself.

"A quick bath, I promise, and then you will have an audience with Clariel," said Artemis. "We shall give you your privacy."

Chia felt her stomach churn. Whoever or whatever Clariel was, would she really be able to help Viola? She wiped the tears forming, curious to see where Artemis would go. He walked up to an enormous oval mirror along the wall, almost the same size as the lake, and casually walked through it, leaving only flower petals to float through the air. Chia was stunned. Jeremy, the wild and worn-out fox, walked after him, looking dazed and disoriented as he emerged from the long twirling slide. He held his little fox fists up in the air. His threat lingered as he disappeared through the liquid mirror after Artemis.

Pip jumped back into her arms with a shriek at the sight of Jeremy's fists. For the first time, Chia had hope in her heart and mind. "Don't worry, little friend. We'll get help and leave soon enough. And I won't let Jeremy eat you. I promise."

She looked around, a bewildered feeling washing over her, at the change of events in just a few small hours. She was at 66 Lilly Pilly Lane, and she felt there were more secrets about this house she was yet to discover. It was as if the house were alive. It was as if it was beckoning her to stay. As if it were her home. For the first time in a long time, Chia felt like she belonged.

5

CLARIEL

Chia looked at the ground, which was still covered generously with moss despite Artemis having left the room. She noticed for the first time that, other than the front door, there were no other doors in this room.

Chia had been so preoccupied thinking about Viola, her newfound vision, and the strange creatures she had met, that she had forgotten to ask where this magic had come from. How was it possible? What more could it do? If Ms. Roberta had brought her here, then could she not also rescue Viola?

Chia walked up to the mirror. Her fingers glided on the smooth surface, not passing through as Artemis had. It was hard and impenetrable. She lingered before it, looking at her reflection. She had never seen herself in a mirror before. She didn't know what she looked like. She didn't know what Viola looked like. They were identical, but she had never seen her. Only felt her face. She leaned in closer and scrunched up her nose, deciding it was too wide and flat for her liking. She jutted her chin forward, not liking how long and pointy it was. And her eyes were dark and boring. She frowned at her reflection and thought once again of Artemis and Jeremy passing through the mirror before her. "How did he do that? Go through the mirror like that?"

"Artemis can do what others cannot," said Heidi.

"You're not just beautiful. You're smart too," said Pip as he gazed at Heidi, love hearts flowing from his eyes.

Chia shook her head at him, itching for someone to answer her questions. "Where does all this magic come from? How is Artemis a talking tree, and Jeremy a talking fox? What is this house?"

"It's 66 Lilly Pilly Lane. It's the most magical place there is. Well, was, before *you know what* happened. Stand back against the wall please, miss. I will summon your bath."

"I'll stand anywhere for *you*," said Pip, tripping over himself and landing in a rose bush filled with thorns. He smiled at Heidi as if he was enjoying the thorns now embedded in his soft down.

Chia picked up her lovesick duck and stood against the wall, wondering what Heidi meant about the house. "What do you mean it *was* magical? Before *what* happened? Tell me more. Please?"

Heidi clicked her bill together in response and flapped her wings wildly, pink dust appearing out of nowhere. Chia coughed, wondering what it was and where it had come from. As she sneezed out the strange powder, an even stranger thing happened. The room spun, not from side to side, but from top to bottom. Still getting used to her eyes, Chia wondered what was happening. Was she being transported somewhere new again? Everything blurred together, creating a kaleidoscope of color.

Just as quickly as it had started, the room was still again. Except now the grass and moss and trees and toadstools were where the ceiling had been. And the body of water and the waterfall were now on the ground.

"Help! I'm dizzy!" cried Pip.

Chia hugged him to her. "It's all right. It's stopped now. Look and see. It's incredible."

"I'll leave you to both to bathe quickly and be back for you in a few minutes." Heidi waddled through the mirror with ease.

Chia dropped Pip, who flew at the mirror with a fierce determination to follow her. But he bounced off it, unsuccessful.

Chia pulled off her red rain boots and jumped into the water with her dress and socks still on. She was never more grateful for water. How divine it was to swim and feel clean again. She had craved it more than she had realized.

Gushes of color bubbled up from the depths of the water and washed over her, removing dirt without her needing to scrub herself clean. "What colors are these, do you know, Pip?"

"Colors? Yes, of course. This one is yellow. This one is orange. Purple. Blue. Brown. Red. This ugly color is pink, like that nasty fox."

"Oh, pink is wonderful. They all are. I've missed a great deal being blind. I'm very happy I can see." Chia had been so overwhelmed with all she had seen, she had forgotten to celebrate that she now could.

She swam through the water, the colors spreading aside for her. She tumbled and flipped, did handstands, and bubbled her way underwater. Little white fish glowed their way past her and tickled her with their fins. She laughed, blowing bubbles through the colors and urging on the little fish. She felt so happy she could burst.

But her sister. Chia needed to keep her focus. What if they'd designed this place to distract her? To get her out of the way. What if Priscilla had somehow organized all of this to get her out of her hair? But Priscilla needed Chia down in the mines to find her precious diamonds. Diamonds Pricilla wanted more than anything. It wasn't possible she had been the one to send her here. Was it?

Her mind was a flurry. She didn't know who to trust. And she didn't know how to trust herself. But she trusted her father. The one memory that was sharpest in her mind was of him telling her to always look after Viola. Chia burst forth from the water, pushing away her pleasure and welcoming back her guilt. She couldn't waste time enjoying herself any longer.

"Pip, we need to get back to work. Our fun is done."

Pip looked out from the water, dropping a little fish from his mouth.

"Pip!"

"What? I'm starving."

"You just ate!"

Pip waddled out of the water and shook off the colors in all directions. "I'm in love, Chia. I've never been more in love. And love makes me hungry! Besides, I'm a little on the thin side, don't you think? No one likes a skinny duck." He shook out his generous tummy and sat on his blossoming bottom.

Chia shook her head at her dramatic friend. She hadn't realized all this time, when Pip couldn't talk, how animated he could be.

"Wow, look at me. And my dress!" Chia had not only dried instantly as she emerged from the water, but her cuts and bruises were healed. Her dress was shining white once again, all the rips mended. She felt restored to brand new: her body, her dress, even her resolve. Everything except her socks, which were still dirty, holey, and now wet. "This place is so magical it frightens me."

"It's wonderful," said Pip, shaking his dried and fluffed bottom into the air. "I've never looked so good."

Just as Chia slipped on her red boots, a loud rumbling sound filled the room, and the water shook and trembled. "It's going back up," said Pip, closing his eyes and squeezing himself against the wall.

The room spun, and within a few seconds, the lake was back on the ceiling and the mossy field on the ground.

"I'm not sure I could ever get used to this. It's like the house has feelings and knows things." Chia was relieved to see Heidi walk back in through the mirror.

Pip sprang to life, somersaulting like he was a seasoned trapeze artist. He landed on his tummy at Heidi's feet, head up, gazing at her adoringly. "My delightful queen. My delicious princess. My dainty duck."

Heidi turned her back on him and announced, "Follow me. Clariel will see you now."

Chia felt the hair on her skin stand up like a ballerina on tiptoes. Electricity rolled up and down her spine. Was she nervous? Excited? Scared? She didn't know who or what Clariel was, but this might be the person who would help her. "Will she bring Viola here for me?"

Heidi kept silent, disappearing through the mirror.

"Wait, come back. We can't go through the mirror," called Chia, desperate to follow her.

Pip bounced up onto his webbed feet and followed Heidi as if under a love spell, melting into the mirror chest-first, and vanishing from sight. The silver moved about like jelly, then reformed still and hard.

Chia swallowed deeply. What would she say to Clariel? How would she convince her to help her sister? Was Clariel a tree too? Or a duck? Or a fox? Or was she a person just like her?

"You're missing out, Chia. It's even better on this side of the mirror!" came Pip's voice from the other side.

Chia gulped in a giant breath of air, holding it in her mouth for courage, and ran through the mirror headfirst, hoping it would welcome her. It was like moving through honey, slow and sticky and slimy. As she emerged on the other side and drank in the sights, she breathed out with shock, delight, and surprise once more.

This side of the mirror looked like a house should look. She was inside a long hall, the walls on either side of her made of wood paneling, with floorboards to match. Chandeliers adorned with sparkling crystals hung from the plaster ceiling. Ornate tabletops, with winged angel statues holding them up, lined the walls on either side and created a welcoming air. Soft mist swirled at her feet. "What color is this?"

"That's gold," said Pip pointing to the statues and the chandeliers and the mist. "Isn't it grand?"

"I've never seen anything so wonderful in my life," she said, running her fingers over the gold statues and through the magical mist.

"Come along. Clariel doesn't like to be kept waiting." Heidi walked solemnly forward.

Chia wondered why she was serious and depressed. This place was so magical and special. What more could anyone want than to live or work here?

She swept Pip up in her arms and followed Heidi to the end of the hall. There was no door. No windows. No escape. Just another mirror identical to the one she had passed through.

"Walk through the mirror, and you will find her on the other side. I'll wait here."

"I'd better wait with you, my love, just in case you get lonely," Pip said. He wobbled from side to side, trying to free himself from Chia's nervous embrace.

But Chia held him firmly. "I think you'd better come with me."

Chia wasn't sure why, but she curtsied to Heidi, closed her eyes, comforted by the darkness, and ambled through the mirror. This one tingled and tangled all over her body, like it was pulling her forward.

She stepped out the other side and opened her eyes. It

was dark. Darker than her own blindness had been. Shivers crept up her spine so suddenly, she wondered if spiders were crawling all over her.

"Chia, I'm scared." Pip's voice was like a small child's whimper.

"Me too, Pip. But we must try to help Viola. Be brave."

A small light appeared in midair, much to Chia's relief, and slowly spread out, illuminating what looked like a giant white sheet, or curtain, hung in the center of a round room. It didn't match what Chia had expected, or the magic of the rest of the house. The sheet looked clumsy hung up like that, and she could make out strings holding it up.

"Welcome," boomed a female voice, crisp and commanding. The sound echoed off the round walls. Pip snuggled his head into Chia's armpit.

"Thank you. I'm here to ask for your help."

"I know what you've come for. I know everything," said the voice.

Chia puffed out her chest and pushed her fear of failure back into the pit of her stomach. She had to ask. But she couldn't find the words she was searching for.

"I ordered Roberta to bring you. You are very important, Chia."

Chia didn't know what she meant. All she could think about was her sister. She was the important one. "I need to help my sister. I need to save Viola from my stepmother. She's kind and good and special. Please, will you help me?"

She took in a giant gulp of air, the last of her courage leaving with her words.

"What makes you think Viola needs or deserves your help or mine?" The voice's vibrations moved the sheet, white and glowing.

"She's my sister. I have to save her."

"But does she deserve it? After all she's done to you?"

Chia gulped down hard, not understanding. Viola had never harmed her. Hitchens lied and nothing more.

"Viola is good. It's Priscilla who is keeping her prisoner." Chia's tone was so high pitched she thought it would tear through the sheet in front of her. She dropped to her knees, still holding Pip to her chest. "I promised my father I would look after her. She's my twin sister. I have to protect her. Will you help me save her?" Chia let her tears and frustration flow for the first time in a long time. She had to succeed. She had to keep her promise.

"Your sister is just as mean and cruel and dangerous as your stepmother." The voice, which had been soft and kind moments earlier, was as sharp as barbed wire. The words cut through Chia's heart like a hot knife through butter.

"She's not. She's kind and generous and better than I am. She would never have run away here and left me behind like I left her. I'm the mean and cruel one."

Silence filled the room. Only Chia's sobs echoed off the round walls imprisoning her. The light grew brighter, the most majestic sight appearing upon the white sheet. Chia rubbed her tears away and gasped. The shadow illuminated upon the sheet looked just like an angel, she decided. Giant wings spread forth from a slender body and filled the white sheet.

"You're an angel! You really can fulfill my wish. You really can. Please, please, you must. I have to save her. She's all I have left in the world."

"Hey, what am I, duck stew?"

"And you, Pip. You're dear to me too."

The shadow of the angel shimmered on the sheet. Silence filled the room once more.

"Yes, I will help you."

Chia stomped her feet happily as Clariel agreed to help her. "Thank you!"

"But you must do something for me."

Chia leaned back, scrunching her forehead. She must do something for Clariel? She shook her head. She was helpless but needed to rescue her sister. She had no time to waste.

"You must return something. Something stolen. Something your stepmother stole."

Chia's mind raced from an image of her stepmother, Priscilla, to this house, to the sheet and shadow of the angel before her. "I don't understand."

"The item your stepmother stole—only you can get it back. I will allow you to leave this house with your sight, and your duck, and with a spell to save Viola. But only if you steal the thing I need from Priscilla."

Chia rocked in place, hugging Pip to her chest more tightly. She couldn't steal something from Priscilla, even with her eyesight. There was no person on Earth she feared more. Priscilla had killed her father. She had neither heart nor soul. She was the most dangerous person alive.

"If you can grant wishes, can you not get what you need from her yourself?" Chia hoped there was another way.

"I cannot. Only you can return what she stole. It must be you."

"What is it? What must I take from her?"

The shadow wings flapped up and down, moving the sheet and creating a stronger breeze. The words were short and sharp. "You must bring me her heart."

Chia coughed violently. Her heart? She could not kill Priscilla. She could not hurt any living soul. "No! I cannot. I will not. I will not kill another person. I am not . . ."

"You are not like Priscilla? No, you are not. But you want to save your sister. If you want to save her, the only way is to bring me Priscilla's heart."

Silence, deafening and still, bounced off the round walls once more, across the sheet, and into Chia's limbs. She wished she could run from this house, which had teased and tempted and taunted her.

She thought of her sister Viola. She was all she had left. Her heart beat fast, her chest heaved, and her stomach hurled. "Yes. I'll do as you ask. I'll bring you Priscilla's heart. I'll do it. For Viola."

6

MAGIC DUST

Chia walked down the hallway, one side of her brain fighting the other over what she should do. She looked at the two small bottles in her hand. Bottles Clariel had given her. Bottles that held power. And pain. One was red, the other purple. The powder inside the red bottle would help rescue her sister Viola. She could use it to make her agree to come with her.

Chia wasn't sure why she would need it. Viola would come with her. She just needed to get past Priscilla to convince her.

The powder inside the purple bottle would let her take Priscilla's heart. One sprinkle of this powder would allow Chia to push her hand inside Priscilla's chest and pull out her heart.

Chia's hand trembled as she clutched a small brown bag in her other hand. Inside it, a heart pulsed as if trying to free itself. All that Chia had to do to be free of Priscilla forever was take out her heart and replace it with the heart in the bag.

Chia's stomach did somersaults and tied itself in knots. She didn't feel especially courageous. Just scared. Very, very scared. She almost preferred the mines, compared with facing Priscilla. But Chia had given her word to Clariel. What would happen to Viola if she didn't keep it?

She squeezed the bottles and bag a little tighter, remembering the feather. Clariel had also given her a feather. It was cherry red with gold edging. Clariel hadn't told her what the feather was for. But Chia felt somehow protected with the feather in her hand. Perhaps it too had some magic.

"What did you think of all that, Pip? You didn't say much when we were in there," Chia whispered as she followed Heidi down the hallway, which seemed curiously longer than when they had walked it the first time, and sloped mysteriously upward.

"Something fishy is going on. There's something Clariel isn't telling us. And what's with hiding behind a giant sheet?" Pip nipped at his duck down with his bill.

Chia's stomach churned with indecision. She had said yes to taking Priscilla's heart, but she needed to be sure it really was the right thing to do. She needed time to think.

Heidi walked through the mirror at the end of the hall, and Chia followed her through. Walking through mirrors seemed commonplace now, although she still preferred doors. This time the mirror felt light and bubbly, like the water she had bathed in earlier.

She gasped. Was there no end to the magic of this

house? She wasn't back in the main room of the house, but inside a generously sized bedroom. In the middle was the biggest bed Chia had ever seen. She was used to sleeping on hard ground. The bed looked like someone had made it for the wealthiest king or queen to sleep on.

"Remind me, is this color pink?" she asked Pip.

"Yep. Blah! As pink as that rotten fox. I would prefer a green room for me, my darling." Pip flew out of Chia's arms and waddled toward Heidi, who looked at the ground instead of at Pip's adoring gaze.

"This is your room. But I can put in a request for a green room for you tomorrow. Enjoy your sleep. I must go," she said, hurrying from the room.

"Please don't go, my darling duck. Spend some time with me. Tell me all about yourself. What's your favorite kind of worm?" Pip lunged at Heidi as he spoke, but she was faster.

She moved back through the mirror, and when Pip attempted to follow her, he bounced off it instead. "Aargh! Looks like we're stuck in here. Prisoners! That's what we are. And I've heard of hard to get, but that duck is ridiculously difficult to romance."

Chia rolled her eyes. She wasn't sure what to make of Pip, her talking, lovesick duck. But she was glad to have a friend by her side. She looked back at the bed, then ran and jumped on it, landing on her back. It was all it promised and more—scrumptiously softer than a pile of hay. Chia rolled on the bed and yelled out in pleasure and relief, mixed with frustration. She still had to decide what to do. She placed the bottles, beating heart, and feather on the ornate wooden bedside table. "What should we do, Pip? Help Clariel or run away from this wickedly wonderful place?"

But when she looked for Pip, he was already curled up at the base of the bed, fast asleep. Glad for Pip's love and devotion, Chia patted her duck and slid under the covers, not bothering to take off her dress. Her decision would have to wait until tomorrow. She stretched her arms out and yawned. The pillow beckoned her to sleep, and she gave in finally, letting a permanent smile paint her face.

Chia woke up from dreaming about colors swirling around in her head. She wondered if she were a giant bird soaring through the sky. Her body was floating and flipping through nothing but air. She was light and calm, strong and supple. A feeling she was not used to. And her mind was as clear as the morning sky. She lay still, not wanting to ruin this perfect moment.

"Did you have a good sleep?"

Chia recognized the voice immediately. It was Ms. Roberta. The woman who had brought her here.

She sat up and opened her eyes, squinting from the light. She wasn't used to the sharp sting of morning light. It was streaming through a large window, bouncing and blending together all the shades of pink in her room.

Chia shook her head in disbelief. So far she had believed that Artemis was a talking, moving tree, and

Jeremy a talking pink fox. But Ms. Roberta was too much for her.

It wasn't possible. Yet there she was in the center of the room, standing ever so relaxed, as if not a care in the world. Except she was . . . a statue. A gold statue. A moving, talking, alive gold statue. She looked like a statue from the hallway that was holding up the tables, only bigger, and without wings. "You're a statue?" Chia yelled, unable to contain her surprise.

Ms. Roberta glistened and gleamed in reply, the sun bouncing off her shiny veneer. A wide smile stretched across her golden face. "I'm very pleased you can see me now. It's very difficult to explain what I am without frightening people. I didn't think you'd understand yesterday when we met. And I'm sorry I ran off on you like that. But I was terribly late."

"To see Robert?" said Chia.

"Yes, Robert."

"Is Robert a statue too?" said Chia.

"Oh no. I'm the only statue around here." Ms. Roberta moved her arms and legs with ease. Her fancy gold dress that draped all the way to the ground moved too, as if it wasn't made of solid gold. And Chia noticed she wore the highest of high heels. Her long golden hair hung all over her shoulders, and despite having a solid-gold face, she was unusually pretty with a small set nose, big round eyes, and full lips.

"You're . . . beautiful," said Chia, not planning to say what she thought out loud.

Pip grunted like he was a horse rather than a duck.

"You'll do for a statue. But where is my love, Heidi?" He sniffed around the room, as if he would smell her out.

"She's hiding from *you*, I think. She's not so fond of ducks, I'm afraid." Ms. Roberta kept a straight face as she talked, not giving much away.

Chia tried hard not to laugh. She didn't want to hurt her duck's feelings. But it all seemed a little silly to her. Ducks in love.

"Not into ducks? I've never heard anything so ridiculous. She's a duck, isn't she? What she needs in her life is a solid, reliable, good-looking duck. I'm just the duck for her." He stood tall and proud on the end of the bed and ruffled up his feathers.

Ms. Roberta gave way and giggled. Chia allowed herself to join in.

"I demand an apology at once!" Pip jumped from the bed and dived into the mirror, only to find himself still captive. "Let me out. Apologize or release me."

"Now, now. I'm sorry I laughed at you." Ms. Roberta knelt down, picked up Pip, and scratched his belly. He turned onto his back in her hands, oohing and aahing in pleasure.

"He's easy to please," laughed Chia.

"Are you ready for some planning?" asked Ms. Roberta, tapping her foot on the floor over and over again very quickly.

"What are we planning for?"

"We're all coming with you. To defeat Priscilla," replied Ms. Roberta.

"You know I'm supposed to steal Priscilla's heart?"

Chia felt her body grow heavy again, tension creeping up her back and neck. She wished she could crawl back under the covers and return to her dream of flying. She glimpsed the bottles and the beating heart, lying on the bedside table.

Ms. Roberta spun on the spot. "I know everything. The house told me. We all know. And we're coming with you!"

The house? Chia wondered why everyone kept referring to the house as if it were a person. She breathed out relief mixed with fear. On the one hand, perhaps it would be easier with a talking tree, a fox, and a gold statue by her side. On the other hand, she still had to face Priscilla.

"What if I can't do it?"

"Don't speak like that. You can. The house has been waiting for you. If it let you in, then it believes in you. We all do."

Chia twirled her hair around her fingers, feeling confused. "What do you mean?"

"You're special. You are the only one who can save us all. I want to tell you more, I really do. But if I do, it will spoil everything. The main thing is you get to help your sister, right?"

Chia wanted to ask many questions. But she decided against it. No one seemed to give her a straight answer, so what was the point? "Yes, she's all that matters to me."

"Come on, then, get dressed. You can't come like that." Ms. Roberta gently placed Pip onto the soft pink carpet and pointed to a neat pile of freshly perfumed clothes on the end of the bed.

Chia nodded in agreement.

"Good! And once you're dressed, just come through the mirror, down the hall, and back into the Haven Room. I'll see you there! Any requests for breakfast?"

"I'll have six dozen eggs, chicken eggs. A large bucket of worms, and a shot of vodka, thank you very much for asking," Pip said without delay.

Ms. Roberta clapped her hands toward Pip. "You're a riot. I'm sure Artemis won't disappoint my hungry feathered friend. Fried, poached, or boiled?"

"Straight up, still in the shells, thank you kindly."

Ms. Roberta laughed into the ceiling, flicked her hair, and skipped from the room in her golden high heels.

Chia put on the green velvet jumpsuit laid out for her. She slipped on the jacket. "This is blue?" she asked, pointing to the jacket.

"Red. You look a little like Christmas wearing that."

"This must be for you to wear." Chia handed Pip a little brown vest. It was made of soft wood woven together.

"I'll feel like a knight in shining armor and will woo my darling Heidi. Is there a sword? I can't go to battle without a sword."

"No sword. But, Pip, we're not going to battle." She carefully placed the two bottles, beating heart, and feather into her pockets. "We'll get Priscilla's heart with this magic powder, save Viola, then leave. That's all we're doing."

"*Hm*, I still don't see why you want to save Viola. But I'll do it for *you*. I'll do anything for you." He waddled toward Chia and rubbed against her leg.

She picked him up, and he nuzzled his head into his favorite spot.

"You're my one true friend," she said.

"Not anymore. You have lots of friends now, and they've all agreed to help you."

Chia sat on the bed thinking about Pip's words. He was right. With the help of her new friends, she might just succeed. How could she possibly fail with the help of a feisty pink fox, a gentle giant tree, a spirited gold statue, and two ducks by her side? She might just pull this off.

7

CHRISTMAS

Chia walked back through the mirror in her bedroom and into the hallway. How did the one hallway always lead somewhere different? It was most unusual.

Yesterday, it had taken her from the main room of the house (the Haven Room as Ms. Roberta had called it) to the round white room to see Clariel. The same hallway had then led to her bedroom. One hallway, many destinations. The house was filled with the most splendid secrets.

She rubbed her face with her green velvet sleeve, enjoying the texture. She was still getting used to having her sight. Her sense of touch and hearing were still stronger and more familiar. They had been all she had to rely on for so long.

"Come on, Pip. The sooner we get this done, the sooner we can find a new place to live. Won't that be wonderful? I'll make sure it will have a lake for you to swim in. We can be happy for the first time!"

"Can I bring Heidi with me? I mean, if she's my wife, I must bring her."

"Focus, Pip. You can fall in love with Heidi later. We have to save Viola and get Priscilla's heart."

Pip made a noise that was a cross between a pig snorting and a buzz of bees protecting their honey. He waddled through the mirror at the end of the hall.

Chia followed him, emerging into the large oasis of the Haven Room. Her skin tingled and her mouth fell open at the dazzling decorations. The Haven Room was eloquently decorated in Christmas colors. Chia looked down at her outfit and felt perfectly at home in her green jumpsuit and red jacket.

Artemis was draped with red-and-gold baubles, and dancing fairy lights glowed through his foliage. The lilly pilly trees were all adorned with tinsel, and there was a large round table set with the most delightful things to eat.

"I guessed you wouldn't mind a Christmas banquet, given it's Christmas today!" Ms. Roberta jumped out from behind Artemis and waved them toward the table. "And I didn't forget you, little duck. Here is your breakfast feast."

Beside the large table was a smaller one piled high with eggs delicately balanced and a plate of wriggling worms.

Pip jumped up and down like a six-year-old. "You have outdone yourself, my lady. But I can't possibly eat this alone. Where is Heidi? And come to think of it, where's my vodka?"

"Some eggnog will do nicely in its place," said

Artemis, serving Pip a large glass before he could argue. Chia noticed that his branches held presents all wrapped in glowing gold paper.

"I can't even remember the last Christmas I had. Is it really Christmas today? Really?" said Chia, feeling bubbles of excitement well up in her tummy.

Jeremy slipped in through the mirror. "You didn't know it was Christmas? So typical. She's uneducated, unpopular, and unwelcome. Throw her out, I implore you, Artemis."

Chia turned away from Jeremy, deciding she would ignore him from now on.

"Hello, Jeremy. You're always a bright ray of sunshine, aren't you?" said Ms. Roberta.

"Help! Save me from that venomous villain. He will eat me for Christmas lunch!" Pip jumped into Chia's arms and hid his head in her armpit as usual, his bottom sticking up into the air, trembling.

"I've decided you're too fat and chewy for my liking. I prefer my duck lean and succulent." Jeremy hopped onto the largest of the toadstools and made himself at home at the Christmas table. He casually picked up a giant leg of roast turkey. "Besides, turkey is much more delicious that nasty old duck meat."

"Fat duck? Chewy duck? Old duck? Why, you . . . ! I'll show you . . ." Pip pulled his head out from Chia's armpit and shook it in threat, but stayed put in her arms.

"Jeremy, that's enough." Artemis gently tapped him on the back of the head. "Mr. Pip, I have had a word or two with Jeremy, and he will not bother you again. Will you, Jeremy?" Artemis spoke softly yet with force.

"No," Jeremy mumbled as he bit into the turkey leg.

Artemis smiled and hit two branches together as if clapping. "I expect you to put your differences aside, Mr. Pip, and get along. We will not win against Priscilla unless we are all united. Now please, everyone, sit and eat. The food is most delicious, I assure you."

Chia placed Pip on the ground next to his breakfast and sat down at the table, which was dressed in a radish-red tablecloth. Star-shaped flower buds of all different colors were scattered in between the food.

She felt her stomach rumble with hunger at the sight of all the food before her. She hadn't eaten properly in weeks, and the few sips of soup she had when she arrived the day before hardly filled her empty stomach. She put aside her manners and helped herself to mashed potatoes, steamed rice, roast pumpkin, and other vegetarian delights. She closed her eyes tight and ate. The flavors flip-flopped on her tongue and coated her throat with sweet, sour, bitter, and salty tastes.

"*Mm.* This is so good." She still preferred to eat with her eyes closed. It made her feel safe, and she could taste everything better. And this was a feast she wanted to remember. "So it really is Christmas?"

"You really didn't know today was Christmas?" said Ms. Roberta. Unable to eat, she stood and looked on as Chia, Pip, and Jeremy shoved food into their mouths like they were starved rhinoceroses.

"Not at all. There were no decorations in the mines.

And I haven't been to the house in . . . I'm not sure. I don't know how long I've been in the mines. Weeks, maybe."

Artemis gave Ms. Roberta a funny look, his eyes moving up and down quickly, and Ms. Roberta returned his look with a solemn nod.

Chia continued. "Hitchens beats me whenever I ask to go home." She swallowed the soft potato and the memories down her throat, washing them away with apple cider.

"Tough gig, kid. He beats you?" Jeremy's voice floated into Chia's ears with such compassion to it, she opened her eyes to check it was really him talking. He looked genuinely sad. It was the first sign of kindness she had seen from the bad-mouthed fox.

"He just slaps me, mostly. One time he used a stick, but only once." She wriggled around in the chair as she remembered how sore her bottom was after that beating. "I try to focus on the good times. Of my father. Of helping my sister, and one day being free. Being happy is what keeps me going."

"But I thought Viola was mean and cruel? That's what I heard," said Jeremy. He took a giant bite into a piece of cherry pie.

Chia knitted her eyebrows together. Why did everyone keep saying that? She was different than Chia, more concerned with clothes and looks than Chia was, but she had always been kind to her. "She can be a little possessive. She never lets me play with her dolls, or wear her clothes. But she's always loved me."

"Your sister sounds like a GIANT HAIRY TARAN-TULA!" Jeremy yelled.

Everyone looked at him like he'd lost his mind.

"Oh no, she's truly not bad, really she isn't," said Chia.

"GIANT HAIRY TARANTULA!" Jeremy pointed behind Chia, his fox paw trembling. He darted under the table, the cherry pie still clutched tightly in his other paw.

Chia turned around slowly. Her heart crept up into her chest and landed with a *thump*. Behind her, a ginormous black-and-yellow spider, with even bigger black-and-yellow eyes, drifted toward them. It was so big it spanned at least a quarter of the room, and squashed several lilly pilly trees as it crept toward them, one hairy step at a time. Its legs reached halfway up the height of Artemis's trunk, and its body was as big as a dinosaur would have been, if not bigger.

Pip quacked and flapped around the room, throwing eggs and worms in all directions. He tried to climb up Artemis's trunk with no success. Chia scooped him up, wondering why her legs wouldn't move despite her instructions for them to run.

"Relax," said Ms. Roberta. "That's Matilda. She's just a harmless tarantula. She won't hurt anyone, will you, my darling?" Ms. Roberta casually strolled up to the spider and patted its ankles, which was as high as she could reach. The spider wiggled about like it was ticklish. "She's our ride to Chia's house," Ms. Roberta continued. "You didn't think I'd make you walk, did you? She's harmless! But watching you three panic was fun!"

Jeremy, still panicking, didn't hear a word Ms. Roberta

said. "Please don't let me die this way," he yelled, rolling himself up so tightly he looked like a ball of pink yarn. "Don't eat me!"

"Ha ha ha! *Quack!* Now you know how I feel! Yes, eat him, please. I'd pay to see that!" Pip jumped down from Chia's arms and waddled under the table, laughing and poking at the terrified fox.

"It's eating me! I'm dying. Goodbye, world." Jeremy rolled onto his back as if something had attacked him. He was shaking so hard and squeezing his fists even harder. Cherry pie dripped all over him.

"Pip, don't be mean. It's all right, Jeremy. Come out. It's a friendly spider. I'm sure it is." Chia glanced at the spider and hoped it really was friendly. It looked dazed and confused. But still terrifying.

Jeremy peeked open one eye, caught sight of the cherry juice all over himself, and screamed, thinking it was blood. "I'm dead. I'm dead. It's all over. My life is done! I've been eaten."

Pip was laughing so hard he rolled around on the moss. "It would be a much nicer world without you in it. I agree. But it's just cherry pie, you goose!"

Jeremy stopped yelling and bounced upright immediately. With a haughty cough, he stood as straight as a small pink fox could, and lifted his chin to the air. "I knew that. I knew all along. Of course I did. I'm fine. Yes, I'm fine. That's a friendly spider. I didn't want the duck to feel stupid. So I played along."

Pip stared at Jeremy with his bill wide open.

"You're welcome," Jeremy said to Pip, jumping back onto his toadstool. "See, Artemis. I can be nice!"

Pip groaned and sat back down to his food, turning his back to Jeremy.

Chia wondered how they would ever set off on their journey with all the bickering between Pip and Jeremy. She wondered why they couldn't go back home the same way they had come—with magic. "Ms. Roberta, why can't you use the same magic you brought me here with to take me home?"

"A fine idea, Chia, but alas, that magic doesn't work on the others because they're . . . well, they're . . . not people. Not the usual people, if you know what I mean?"

Chia stared at her. Ms. Roberta, who was usually so confident and self assured, looked uneasy. She had stopped patting the spider and was playing restlessly with her necklace. Her feet zig-zagged from side to side. There was something she wasn't telling Chia.

"What are you all? Why are you a statue, and Artemis a giant tree, and Jeremy a pink fox? How do you have magic, and why does everyone keep referring to the house as if it were a person?" Chia paused, sucking in a big breath of air. "And why haven't the neighbors complained about you all?"

Ms. Roberta glimpsed at Artemis, twisting her beaded necklace so hard it would have popped apart had it not been made of gold. "Neighbors? Oh, there are no neighbors. The houses around this one are all empty."

Artemis allowed the presents he was holding to drop onto the soft dewy moss. "Once we defeat Priscilla, we will explain everything, I promise. But until then you will need to trust us."

Chia sat on a toadstool, her body stiffening. She didn't feel like eating anymore despite the growls coming from her stomach. Her throat was dry, and her eyes stung. She blinked back her tears, an image of Viola coming into her mind. It didn't matter that her mind was fluttering with curiosity. It didn't matter who these creatures were. All that mattered was that they would help her save Viola.

"Open your present," said Ms. Roberta, handing Chia a large parcel and lifting the mood.

Chia pressed her open palms to her heart. She had a present. She hadn't gotten a present in . . . well, it had been a long time. Since before her father had married Priscilla. Her memory was a little patchy. Or was it even longer than that?

Chia was very grateful. She unwrapped it slowly, carefully, piece by piece, savoring the moment.

"Woo hoo! Look at me. I got a gun!" said Pip, racing around in a circle with what looked like a gun held tightly in his bill.

"Pip! Put that down. Why did you give him a gun?" Chia dropped her gift and tried to take the gun from Pip. He mumbled something she couldn't understand and held his grip.

"Don't panic. It is no gun." Artemis swayed from side to side, his big blue eyes widening even more at the twittering duck before him.

Pip dropped the gun-looking object. He put the tips of his wing where his hips should have been and looked into Artemis's eyes. "You tricked me. I don't have fingers to use a gun."

Artemis laughed with merriment. "It has no trigger, so fingers would be of no use. This is a Mind Weaver."

"You gave him a Mind Weaver! Him?" Jeremy let go of the giant piece of ham he was busy eating and scampered up to Artemis's face. "Really?"

Artemis held Jeremy's gaze. "Pip is the perfect one to use it. It's his present, and it belongs to him now."

"What does it do?" Chia picked up the brown T-squared object that looked very much like a gun without a trigger.

No-one answered her. Instead Pip did a little dance at the base of Artemis's trunk, far enough away from the raging fox to be safe. "Ha ha! Suck it up, pinky! I got the Mind Weaver. Not you!"

Jeremy looked like he was about to jump on Pip and eat him in one mouthful.

"Don't mind Pip. Open your present, Jeremy." Artemis shooed the little fox away from him. "I think you will be pleased. And no more eating for you. Matilda can't carry so much weight, and you weigh more than a baby whale given all you've eaten."

Jeremy scowled at him and scuttled to a small package. He ripped the paper open like a small child eager to see what he got. "*Hm.* It's nice," he grumbled, taking out a tiny pair of yellow pants and squeezing them on. "At least I've got style."

Artemis lifted him up to one of his branches. "To answer your question, Chia, a Mind Weaver allows you to change people's minds. To help them see things your way."

Chia twirled the Mind Weaver around in her hand. This could come in very handy. But she knew it belonged to Pip. She handed it to him, feeling pangs of envy.

Pip waddled away in excitement as he took the Mind Weaver. He dropped it onto the grass so he could talk. "How do I make it work if it has no trigger?"

"You point it toward someone and think what you want the person you're aiming at to think," said Ms. Roberta, picking it up and handing it back to Pip. "It's as easy as that. They will think as you want them to, at least for a short time. But it can only be used once on each person, so use it wisely, little duck. Try it."

Pip took the Mind Weaver back into his bill and pointed it at Jeremy, who scampered down from Artemis's branches and hid behind a teepee. "Don't you dare!"

Pip flapped his wings teasingly and then moved and pointed the Mind Weaver toward Artemis, who just stared back at him with no expression on his tree face.

"*Hm.* Try it you say. I can make anyone think whatever I want them to? Just like that?" said Pip, his bill still holding tight to the Mind Weaver as he talked.

"Yes, just like that," repeated Ms. Roberta.

Pip pointed the Mind Weaver at her as she spoke. "Fine. Here goes!"

Chia wondered what Pip could want Ms. Roberta to think. She was already level headed, kind, helpful. But then she spotted Heidi coming through the mirror. Oh no! Pip was going to—

It was too late. A bright orange light streamed out of the Mind Weaver, crisscrossing its way across the garden and scorching toward Heidi like lightning, its target in sight.

Heidi strolled along, looking at the ground as she always did, oblivious to what was headed right for her.

"Love me, love me, love me!" chanted Pip.

Chia covered her mouth with her hand. She was too far away from Heidi to do anything, and the words to warn her just weren't coming. Everyone else was in a silent stupor too. Just watching. Watching as the orange light got closer and closer to Heidi. She looked up at the very last minute as the light entered both her eyes. She leaned back slightly as if about to fall, but then recovered herself and looked dazed for a moment. Pip waddled up to her so fast it was as if Jeremy had threatened to eat him again.

Heidi leaned backward again, and just as she was about to touch the ground, Pip swept in and caught her, his wings outstretched as if he were half-human, half-duck.

"Heidi, my love?" he asked.

"Yes, my darling. I think, I . . . well, I think I may . . ." Heidi cleared her throat with a loud quack. "I love you!"

"Now do you see why giving that thing to the duck is the single stupidest thing you've ever done?" Jeremy stared at Artemis with rage in his face.

But Artemis just chuckled. "No harm done, is there? Heidi already had a crush on Pip, I'm sure."

Chia couldn't believe her eyes as Pip and Heidi, both

gleaming with happiness, waddled toward them, wing in wing. Apparently completely in love.

"Why can't we use the Mind Weaver on Priscilla? She can give us her heart," said Chia. If it could convince Heidi to love Pip so easily, getting Priscilla's heart would be a cinch.

"First of all, it belongs to Pip. But for reasons we cannot yet explain to you"—Artemis cleared his throat—"it must be you, and you alone, who takes Priscilla's heart. You cannot use the Mind Weaver to trick her."

Chia wanted to ask why, but something stopped her. A tension began in her shoulder and crept its way up her neck, settling at the back of her head. There were strange rules to all this magic she didn't understand, and she knew, given how secretive Artemis was being, she wouldn't get her answer. Not yet.

Ms. Roberta picked up Chia's half-unwrapped present and handed it to her. "You haven't finished opening your gift yet. Go on. You will love it."

Chia gulped down her confused feelings and took it in her arms. Perhaps her present might help her steal Priscilla's heart. She wished there were some way out of it, but as she looked into the hopeful eyes of Ms. Roberta and Artemis, she felt heavy with duty. She had to trust them. She rolled her shoulders and twisted her neck left and right. She ripped away the paper, hoping it was something magical enough to make up for her lack of courage.

8

GIFTS

Chia couldn't believe she was unwrapping a gift. A gift just for her. She felt ever so grateful as she quietly ripped away the many layers of paper. "Who is this from, exactly?"

"It's been in your family forever," said Ms. Roberta.

"Roberta!" Artemis frowned at her.

Chia was positive she saw a tinge of red spread across Ms. Roberta's gold cheek bones.

"Never mind who it's from. It's yours now. That's what matters," said Ms. Roberta, fluttering her long eyelashes so fast they looked like butterflies about to launch.

Chia squinted at her. This present had been in her family? Had it belonged to her father? She ripped off the rest of the paper in one giant piece, the present lying still on the grass, waiting to be picked up. It looked like a large wooden frame of something or other, and at first, she couldn't work out what it was. But then she saw the brown bag full of sharp red arrows. It was a bow-and-arrow set.

"It's wonderful, but I don't know how to use it. And I

would never hurt another living being. Never. Who did you say this belonged to?" She stood up and pushed the bow and arrows away with her red rain boot.

"This is no ordinary bow," said Artemis. "These arrows are the bringers of truth. Whoever you shoot these special arrows at must tell the truth. They do not hurt anyone. They could never." Artemis swayed softly, his eyes glowing with dewdrops. Or were they tears?

"I don't think I could use this. I mean, I really can't," insisted Chia.

Ms. Roberta picked up the bow and held it toward Chia. "Just try it. I think you'll surprise yourself. Your mother was great at . . . oh dear!" Ms. Roberta dropped the bow and covered her mouth with both hands, looking at Artemis with eyes wide open.

The lines of wood all along Artemis's brow line furrowed so deeply that his eyes almost sank into his trunk.

Chia's mind raced. Her mother? What did they know about her mother? She pushed away the urge to pick up the plate in front of her and throw it across the garden. She wasn't sure where this sudden gust of rage had come from. She was normally so good at controlling her temper.

She held her breath and counted to ten. It worked. Her heart stopped beating like a broken clock and thumped at a natural rhythm again. Her mind settled down like wind tired after a long storm. How could this magical bow have belonged to her mother? Her mother had died a long time ago. She couldn't remember her.

Jeremy stopped eating. Pip stopped cuddling Heidi. Ms. Roberta froze, looking like a common garden statue. Matilda woke up from her dozing. The mood turned solemn and thick, and a layer of frost suddenly formed on the trees as if to capture the mood.

Artemis broke the silence. "It is true. This bow belonged to your mother. And while I know you want to know more, I'm sorry, I cannot tell you anything else. There is too much at stake. If you care for your sister, you will be patient. I once again promise you, I will tell you everything . . . just not yet." Artemis glided across to Chia, face to face with her. "We want the best for you Chia. Please believe me."

Chia sucked back her tears and braced her shoulders. She couldn't help but trust Artemis despite him not telling her what she longed to know. "You promise you'll tell me everything? Everything."

Artemis closed his eyes. His words fluttered like dried autumn leaves on the breeze. "I promise."

Chia couldn't hold her tears back as she thought about her mother. She looked at the bow and arrows through her hazy vision. "I killed my mother. She died giving birth to me and Viola. And I don't think she'd like me to have her bow and arrow set."

Chia collapsed onto the moss, her tears wetting the soft velvet of her jumpsuit. A mixture of grief, guilt, and anger flooded her head and heart. She felt suddenly tired and weak.

"Don't cry, Chia, *quack*." Pip nuzzled up against her leg.

Soft leaves stroked her back as Artemis swayed his sympathy toward her. And Ms. Roberta's cold metal cheek met her own.

"I'm sorry, dear dove. It's been so hard without your mother. I should have been more sensitive." Ms. Roberta's words made Chia's muscles relax. She breathed out her tangled mess of memories.

"Can't we tell her the truth, Artemis, please?" Ms. Roberta pleaded. "Just this, nothing else."

Chia peered out from her hands.

"Roberta. We discussed this," said Artemis.

"Yes, but I think it would help Chia. I don't think it would ruin anything to tell her how her mother really died."

Chia pushed Ms. Roberta and Pip aside, and stared up at Artemis, her eyes pleading for the truth. "Please, if you know anything about my mother, tell me."

The soft Christmas music turned off, as if on cue. Everyone stared at her, the silence extending even to the lake and usually gushing waterfall.

Artemis closed his big eyes, the lids vanishing into the bark. He seemed to be thinking. His mouth breathed out heavily as if he was tired and worn out with the responsibilities he had been carrying. "Very well."

Ms. Roberta clapped, then picked up both of Chia's hands. "You didn't kill your mother, Chia. Priscilla did."

Chia's heart raced like a gorilla running through a jungle. Her thoughts felt tangled and knotted and bruised. She had spent her whole life believing she had caused her mother's death, and in a matter of seconds, all that was no longer true. She felt strangely relieved. So relieved. Like who she believed she had been all her life had suddenly changed.

"How?"

"I can't tell you that part, not yet," said Artemis, breathing out a golden glow of breath. "But I promise we'll tell you everything after—"

"You'll tell me after I have taken Priscilla's heart? Fine." Chia wiped the tears from her face, a hatred replacing the sadness.

Priscilla.

She had even more reason to hate her now. She didn't have to believe what Ms. Roberta was saying, but she knew in her gut it was true. Priscilla had killed not only her father, but her mother too. And Chia had spent her whole life feeling like it was her own fault. So many lies. So many things Priscilla had done to hurt her family. What would she do to Viola? Chia scrunched her nose, thinking of Priscilla's face, and picked up the plate filled with strawberry cheesecake. She swung the plate backward and then lunged forward.

"No! Not the cheesecake. Please, not the cheesecake," Jeremy squealed, sounding more like a mouse than a fox.

The plate hit a tree and split into two perfect halves, while the cheesecake landed in one piece on an island of moss. The ants raced for their lives, hungry for dessert, but Matilda the spider was faster and downed the whole thing in one mouthful.

Chia picked up her bow and arrows. "I'm ready to go

now. Let's get Priscilla's heart and end this. I will do whatever it takes." Her voice trembled, and she had a headache.

"Chia, I'm sorry," said Artemis. "We will tell you the rest. I promise."

Chia pursed her lips and slung the bow and arrows over her shoulder, like she was a seasoned hunter rather than a twelve-year-old child. "It doesn't matter right now. I get it. Tell me what to do. So long as I save Viola, that's all that matters."

The shimmering lake above their heads wobbled and shook. The waterfall stopped flowing. Chia felt the temperature become colder again, just as gentle snowflakes fell on them.

"It's like the house is sad," said Chia. She looked at the others, but they turned away from her.

"It wants you to be safe is all," said Heidi. She kissed Pip and then waddled away back through the mirror.

"Wait, my darling, come back," called Pip. But he stayed put beside Chia.

"Don't mind the house. She can get emotional sometimes," said Ms. Roberta. She jumped on Matilda, who lowered her tummy to the ground so they could more easily climb on. Artemis picked up Jeremy and popped him on Matilda's back.

Chia carefully climbed aboard, the spider's hairy legs tickling her. Sitting on the spider's back felt like the mattress she had slept on last night, soft and springy.

"Come on, Pip. Jump. We've wasted enough time." Chia offered her arm for the duck to use as a ramp.

"I can't go anywhere without Heidi. I won't. Not without her, I refuse."

"Truth is she hates you," laughed Jeremy. "And no Mind Weaver will change that. Besides, she needs to stay here and clean your giant mess." Jeremy leaned back on Matilda's head like he was on a sofa couch.

Pip ignored him and continued to call out. "Heidi. Heidi! Please, my divine beauty. My queen of queens. The fire of my heart. The joy of my feathers."

"Quite the poet, your little duck friend," said Ms. Roberta.

"Quiet the pain in the—"

"Jeremy!" Artemis hushed the little fox with a branch and swung Pip onto the spider with another one. Chia grabbed onto him, holding him tight.

Ms. Roberta patted the duck, leaving small indentations in his feathers. "We won't be long, I promise. Just a few hours there and back, maybe less. Heidi will clean up and be here when we get back."

"Fine." Pip broke free of Chia's arms and sat on the tail end of Matilda, on the far side of Jeremy.

"Hold on tight. We will take the shortcut to Chia's house." Artemis waved all his branches at once as if conducting an orchestra.

Chia wondered how they would exit through the small front door, and how it was at all possible for them to travel to her house in a few hours, let alone not be seen. Traveling on a giant tarantula spider was a little peculiar.

As Artemis waved his branches wildly, the mirror that had led to all the different rooms melted away, leaving only its golden frame. No hallway was on the other side this time. Just darkness and fog.

"We will travel by the underground tunnel. It is much safer and faster than any other method," said Artemis.

"We'll get there quickly with Matilda," said Ms. Roberta.

"Does Priscilla know about these tunnels?" asked Chia.

Ms. Roberta looked at her strangely. Her left golden eyebrow raised up, then lowered again. "She does. But she can't access them. The house won't let her."

Chia breathed out in relief. Priscilla had always made her feel scared. Terrified. But she never knew why exactly. Yes, she was particularly cruel to her. But it was more than that. It was as if she knew Chia, had always known Chia, and had decided she didn't like her, even before they met. She shivered thinking about the history she knew nothing about. The history that Priscilla was a part of. If it were true, and Priscilla had killed her mother, there must have been a reason. Priscilla did nothing without reason.

Artemis lowered himself into the tunnel and whizzed away out of sight. Matilda followed him, plunging them into darkness. Chia felt the speed of excitement and adventure move through her bones, muscles, and every cell of her body. She felt alive. Exhilarated. And terrified. Especially terrified.

9

VIOLA

Chia was used to darkness. It neither scared her nor overwhelmed her. Darkness was all she could remember. It felt comfortable to be back in the solitude. She had loved the imagery that danced through her eyes for the last day, but darkness felt like traveling with an old friend as she set off on this journey. A journey to save her sister. A journey to get Priscilla's heart. A journey to change her life.

She wiped her clammy hands on her jacket and jiggled her legs to the melodic symphony of Artemis swaying and Matilda's tender feet tapping their way through the tunnel.

No one spoke.

It felt like at least an hour had passed. Still no one spoke.

Chia breathed in the smells. Dampness. Darkness. And lavender. Lavender? It reminded her of her sister. Oh, how Viola loved lavender. She would always pick the flowers in the bloom of summer and put them throughout the whole house, spreading their sweet scent.

"Viola?" she called, as if expecting her to answer. She breathed more deeply and confirmed with her mind what her nose already knew to be true. The smell was getting stronger and stronger. It was definitely lavender.

"Stop. Stop! I think Viola is here," said Chia.

"Stop." Jeremy's voice echoed off the walls. "Stop, you no-good spider."

Matilda came to a standstill.

"What's the matter, Chia?" said Pip.

Chia sniffed the air like a hound hunting for rabbits. There was the lavender smell again, stinging its way up her nose. "I can smell lavender."

"And? What's the big deal about that?" said Jeremy, licking his pink fur. "We haven't got all day. Get moving again, spidy."

Matilda moved forward.

"No, please stop!" Chia yelled at the top of her lungs. "It's my sister. She's here. She's in here."

"Your sister's in the tunnels? I think you've lost the plot," said Jeremy.

"Chia, your sister couldn't be in the tunnels. Could she?" Ms. Roberta sounded as if she might half believe her.

"I can smell lavender, and Viola always wears lavender perfume. It's definitely her. She's here."

Jeremy sniffed the air, as did Pip and Matilda.

"I can't smell a thing," said Pip.

"Me neither. All I can smell is dampness and spider poop," said Jeremy.

"I know what I'm smelling. I'm right," Chia insisted.

"Artemis is ahead of us. Let's catch up to him and see if what you say is true," said Ms. Roberta.

"Viola is crazy. If she's here, we're all in trouble," Jeremy whispered to Ms. Roberta.

"Let's catch up to Artemis and then decide," said Ms. Roberta.

Chia frowned at them. Why did they keep insisting her sister was bad? Chia turned her back to them, annoyed but not giving up. Her nose was right. She was sure. And as Matilda moved faster, her stomach grew giddy and her sense of smell increased yet again. So much lavender filled it, she felt like she was in a lavender field. She couldn't possibly be imagining it.

Matilda came to a sudden standstill, skidding across the hard ground and flinging everyone off her back. Seconds before hitting the cold hard ground, Chia felt something wrap around her waist. Artemis. She surrendered, drifting upward, happy to have the perfect view as the darkness lifted. But unhappy and overwhelmed with the sight of soldiers. Ten of them, dressed in formal black uniforms and silver helmets, and holding matching silver swords, were marching toward them. Priscilla's guards.

Chia screamed. The sight of the men made her blood feel as though it clogged inside her veins. She felt dread. And despair. And disgust as she remembered them dragging her into the mines, and away from her home. She looked around, glad at least that her friends were all held safely by Artemis's big broad branches.

"Stop, men!"

Chia recognized her sister's voice immediately. As the soldiers came to a standstill, Viola stepped forward.

"You're here. I knew it was you." Chia was so relieved.

"Quick, Chia, the bottle," Jeremy yelled from his branch.

Chia fumbled in her pocket for the bottle of powder she was to use on her sister. Her fingers felt slimy and slippery, and she couldn't be sure which bottle was which.

She was annoyed that Jeremy thought her sister was bad. She wasn't. Viola was good despite what anyone else thought of her.

"Chia. Thank goodness it's you." Viola stepped into the light of the lanterns carried by the soldiers. Wearing a ruby red ballroom gown, she looked very out of place in the dark and dingy tunnel.

"We came to help you. Your dress . . . it's beautiful," said Chia, overwhelmed at seeing her sister for the first time. She looked just like Chia, except her nose seemed a little more upturned, and her hair was long and silky.

"You can see?" said Viola.

Chia nodded.

"Chia, you know how important it is to get what you promised." Artemis's soft, supportive voice reminded Chia that finding Viola was only half of her mission. She still had to face Priscilla.

"Chia, you can't trust Viola!" Pip flapped his wings so hard, Artemis let him go. He sailed through the air and lunged toward Viola. She moved aside, allowing Pip to hit one of the lanterns. He spun about in the air and rebounded into Viola's arms.

"You're so cute. Your duck can talk now?" Viola didn't seem the least offended by his accusation.

Pip looking dazed and confused at what had just happened and quacked at the top of his lungs.

"Oh, he's beyond cute. He's adorable. He doesn't like me much though. Here." Viola handed Pip to Chia just as Artemis was bringing her to the ground.

"Tell your men to back off or we'll ninja them!" Jeremy did somersaults in the air, still safely held up by Artemis.

"We do not trust you," conceded Artemis.

"Let us pass," ordered Ms. Roberta.

Chia cradled Pip with one hand, the other still fumbling for the bottle in her bag. She blew out hard and stomped her foot, giving up on it. Her nerves were stretched to the limits. She was dripping in sweat. Soaked from her fingertips to her feet. Her new friends were against Viola. They still didn't believe her. She turned to face them.

"You're all convinced Viola is bad, but she isn't. She's always been on my side. It wasn't her that put me in the mines. It was Priscilla. Tell them, Viola."

Viola made a circle in the air with her hand. The soldiers took three steps back. "I am here to help you defeat Priscilla. These soldiers are loyal. They serve me. I came to find my sister so I could help her."

Chia gave her friends the angriest face she could muster.

"We don't believe you, you evil imposter," said Jeremy. "You may look all nice and happy, dressed in rosy red, but you're rotten to the core!" Jeremy threw himself headfirst into one of the guards, bouncing off his helmet and landing back on the giant spider.

"Jeremy, you nasty spiteful fox. You've said nothing kind from the moment I met you, and now you're being mean to my sister."

"Chia. Viola cannot be trusted." Artemis's words cut through the air and through Chia's heart. How could he say that? He didn't know her. He knew nothing about her life.

Chia took a large step back from her friends, coming to stand next to Viola. "My sister is good, and if you don't believe me, then I think you need to go back. I don't need you anymore."

Viola raised her eyebrows, put her arm around Chia, and nodded her head in agreement.

Pip looked up at Chia with half the energy of his usual self. "They're right, Chia. She's not who you think she is."

Chia looked down at Pip. She wanted to throw him onto Matilda, but she picked him up and hugged him to her chest tightly. "You don't know what you're saying. None of you do. Maybe you're all under a spell. Maybe Priscilla got to you all. But I know what I've lived. There has never been a day in my life, ever, where my sister has been anything but good to me."

Viola beamed, her perfect white teeth almost catching the light. She looked identical to Chia in every way except she was more regal. Neater perhaps. Cleaner. And an inch taller.

"Whatever you're here to do, tell me and I will help

you." Viola lowered her high-pitched voice, speaking ever so softly.

"We'll tell you nothing!" said Jeremy. "Chia, use the bottle!"

"The bottle?" said Viola.

Chia turned away from Jeremy, squinting her face at him. "Never mind. It's nothing important."

Viola seemed happy enough with that answer. She fanned her arms out and addressed the others. "I know you all don't trust me, but I swear it, I am here to help. I will prove to you I am on your side. My only wish is to help my sister."

"*Pfft!*" Jeremy spat through the air.

"We have no choice but to believe you." Artemis spoke each word especially slowly, cautiously. "We will follow you if you can lead us to Priscilla. There you may prove your loyalty. There you will have a chance to help your sister."

"Yes, of course I will. I would do anything for her."

"You didn't rescue her from the mines. I did," said Ms. Roberta. Chia had never heard her use a strained voice until now. Not even to Jeremy.

Viola flicked her hair from side to side and squeezed Chia more firmly to her. "I was coming for her. When I heard she had already escaped, I came here to the tunnels to look for her."

"Sucked in, Chia. Seriously, you're not going to fall for this, are you?" Jeremy licked his pink fur.

"If what you say is true, order your soldiers to throw

down their weapons." Artemis spoke firmly and forcefully.

"Yes. Men, drop your weapons. Now!" Viola ordered them with ease, and they all did as they were told.

Chia pushed the bit of tension in her stomach away and quieted her mind. Everything was turning out better than expected.

"Well, let us proceed." As Artemis gave the order, everyone climbed back onto Matilda's back, including Viola. Her men turned and marched back from the direction they came from, followed by Artemis, and then the rest.

Chia refused to let her happy disposition be ruined by her friends' misguided feelings toward Viola. They would find out soon enough she was just the same as her—kind, friendly, fun. And loyal.

Viola spread out her dress, taking up over half the space for herself. "Aren't you going to introduce me to your friends?"

Chia was pleased to. "The little pink fox is Jeremy. He's moody and mean."

Jeremy scowled. "Who you calling little? Artemis, I say we dump them both and do this ourselves!"

"You are adorable. You'd make a fine pet," said Viola, petting him like he was a cat. Jeremy recoiled in horror and cuddled up to Pip for protection.

"And this is Ms. Roberta. She's a gold statue."

"Yes, I can see that. Glad to meet you."

Ms. Roberta smiled back coldly without speaking.

"And the tree is Artemis. He works for Clariel. They all

do. She sent us to steal Priscilla's heart and to save you. I came to save you, Viola."

"So you want Priscilla's heart?" Viola's voice was a little wiry and unsure.

Chia clenched her teeth, hoping Viola would still agree to help them.

"Chia will take Priscilla's heart and bring it back to Clariel." Ms. Roberta spoke with no emotion. It was completely unlike her. Chia was annoyed her friends still didn't believe her. That they still didn't believe Viola.

"I can help you. I can lead you straight to her. There is no way to get past her soldiers without me. It's your lucky day." Viola jumped up and down on the spider's back, clapping her hands together.

Chia felt her fear drop right out of her body. With Viola's help, it would be easier. Far, far easier. She would have been happy to escape right now with her sister by her side, but she had to keep her promise to Clariel. And to escape the clutches of Priscilla once and for all.

"We're only about ten minutes from the castle." Viola lay down on the spider and closed her eyes. "Wake me up when we get there. I'm exhausted from so much dancing."

Chia wondered what Viola meant by castle. Her house was a small, simple cottage, not a castle.

Jeremy took the moment of Viola's distraction to lean in close to Chia. "Why not use an arrow on her and find out for real if she's good or bad? She could be leading us into a trap."

Chia leaned away from him. Use a magic arrow on her sister? She knew her sister. Something connected them in a special way. She was good. She had only ever been good. She wanted to say all this, but instead she said, "I don't know how to use a bow and arrow."

Something ticked Chia's cheek. It was dark once more, but she could make out Artemis now traveling beside them. "I think it's time you learn how. And there's no better time than now. Jeremy's right. There's no harm in using it sooner rather than later."

Chia felt excited to learn how to shoot arrows. But the knot in her stomach that continued to grow despite her best efforts to ignore it worried her slightly. She didn't know why. Her battle was half won. She had already found Viola, and she would make the rest easy. All that was left to do was take Priscilla's heart, and it would all be over.

"I can't shoot an arrow while traveling this fast."

"If you can shoot the arrows when traveling, you can shoot them when still," said Artemis. "Now steady your arm, place the arrow into the slot—yes, that's it. Turn your body slightly sideways, and—yes, well done, you're a natural. Now pull back gently and aim for my nose.

"Won't it hurt you?"

"Not at all."

Ms. Roberta moved Chia's arms slightly down away from her shoulders. She felt tense. What if she missed and hit one of the others?

"Pull back gently and focus your mind on Artemis's nose," guided Ms. Roberta. "These arrows follow your thoughts, not your sight. And they don't hurt. They're magical arrows of truth."

Chia pulled back a little more at the tight string and closed her eyes. She imagined Artemis's big woody nose in her mind. It was like she and the bow were one. Tingling coursed through her arms to her pinky toes. Their hearts seemed to beat as one. She released the string and opened her eyes, trying to see if she had hit her target. The arrow was sitting right in the center of Artemis's nose.

"Well done, Chia. You are trained and ready," said Ms. Roberta.

"Just like that?"

"Just like that," said Artemis. "Now all you need is the courage to use the bow and arrows to find the truth once and for all. But it has to be you who chooses it."

Chia wondered what Artemis meant. She would use the bow and arrow on Priscilla with no hesitation. But she wasn't so sure she would ever use it on her friends. And never would she agree to use it on Viola. She trusted her explicitly.

10

THE HEART

The light came pouring in as the tunnel lifted upward, finishing inside what looked like a giant dungeon. Cold stone walls lit by hundreds of large flickering torches made the place feel like it was haunted and eerie.

"Are we here? Is this it?" Chia's feet wobbled inside her red boots. She zipped up her matching red jacket. It was time to face Priscilla. And she didn't feel at all prepared.

"Yes. This is the castle. The Christmas ball is underway, but Mother, I mean Priscilla, was lying down in her room with a headache." Viola stroked her face as if she had been through the most tiring ordeal. She stretched her arms out, almost knocking Pip and Jeremy off Matilda. Then she patted at her arms as if she were clearing away spiderwebs. "Your tree and statue and duck will have to stay here. The statue will draw undue attention, and the tree won't fit. I'm curious how it even fits inside the dungeon."

Chia flinched at the sound of Viola calling Priscilla her

mother. She would never be her mother. She would never be *their* mother. Their mother was Lilly, and she was dead.

She looked at Artemis. He seemed smaller somehow. Sullen even. His big blue eyes looked more gray than blue. Was he not happy? The plan was going better than expected.

Jeremy half snorted and half coughed. "I suppose you want me to stay here too then? Don't want a pink fox drawing any *undue attention* to you. What with that giant red parachute dress you're wearing. No attention at all." Jeremy scrunched his fox face up into the tightest ball ever and stuck out his little pink tongue at Viola.

"I'm so pleased you agree with me. Come, Chia, we only have a small opening of time before the Count arrives, and then Pricilla will need to get back to the ball, headache or not."

Chia was glad for Viola, but she still needed her friends along with her, especially Pip. "I think Ms. Roberta, Jeremy, and Pip should come with us," said Chia softly.

"Nonsense!" Viola's voice sounded impatient and irritable. "We don't need them. I can get Priscilla's heart for you. She won't suspect me. Then I'll hand it to you. Do you have the replacement heart?" Viola offered her perfect manicured hand for the heart.

Chia felt the heart in her pocket beat faster as Viola talked about it. She hadn't mentioned a replacement heart to Viola, had she?

Pip pulled his head out of Chia's armpit, where he had kept it for the last few minutes, puffed out his chest, and bounced forward on the spider toward Viola. "No! She won't give it to you. We're all coming with you, and we'll take the heart from Priscilla ourselves. If you're on our side, you'll take us there."

Viola scratched at her neck, leaving red lines. "Yes, fine. I just thought it would be easier. I'm good either way. I am on your side. Really, I am." She led the way, walking fast, and her men followed behind her like obedient baby ducklings, their combined footfalls echoing off the walls.

Ms. Roberta, Jeremy, and Pip followed too, looking very pleased they could come. Jeremy kept asking Pip if he had any relatives he could eat instead of him.

Chia stayed behind a moment and hugged Artemis to her. "Please, won't you come too, Artemis? I'll feel safer with you there."

"I believe in you, Chia. You will do what's right. I will stay here and guard the tunnel. It is far too important to leave unmanned. And our spider friend might run back without us."

Chia's shoulders slumped. Did she know what was the right thing to do? She was about to steal a person's heart. Granted, it was Priscilla's, a person who had only done bad things to her, but still a person. "Will everything be all right? Once we have Priscilla's heart, will this all be over?"

Artemis breathed out heavily. "I hope so. I do hope so. Here, take this in case you need it." He shook his trunk, allowing a long bristly piece of paper bark to fall from him. Chia leaned down slowly, as if she were a turtle with all the time in the world. She wondered why she would need food. She would have the heart and be back within the hour.

"It doesn't just give you food. It gives you courage." Artemis said no more, turning away from her to face the tunnel entrance.

Chia wanted to ask him what he meant, but Pip waddled back into the dungeon. "Come on, Chia. Hurry up. I don't like being alone with that fox."

Chia scooped Pip up in her arms, tightened her stomach, and lifted her chin. She could do this. She *would* do this. She grasped Pip tightly, and the paper bark even tighter, and headed after the others.

As Chia caught up to Ms. Roberta and Jeremy, she noticed they looked more nervous than she felt. Ms. Roberta turned to Chia. "This castle is very impressive. But it isn't real."

"I believe you," said Chia as she marched up hundreds of steps that she'd never seen before. "It wasn't like this when I lived here. And that was only a few weeks ago, I think. Or months. I can't quite remember how long I've been gone. Did magic do this?"

"Yeah, yeah, magic." Jeremy sulked like a common garden rat. "It's those diamonds you've been digging for her. She's no right to them." He poked out his tongue and ate a fly, looking more like a frog than a fox.

The crunching noise made Chia squirm. That and the information she was digesting. The diamonds Priscilla had made her mine were magical?

They reached the top of the stairs, finding themselves in a large courtyard filled with huge pots of lavender flowers. Perfectly trimmed grass sat in the center. Chia marveled at the castle that stood before them. It definitely wasn't her little house on the hill anymore. Priscilla's new castle was made of glass. It looked like a giant diamond, gleaming and glinting light into her eyes.

"It's magnificent," said Ms. Roberta.

"Thank you. Yes, it's exquisite. We like it," said Viola, sticking her nose into the air as if she herself had just finished building it.

"It looks tacky if you ask me," Jeremy said loudly. "No style whatsoever."

"For once I agree with the heathen." Pip looked around with a sour expression.

Viola and her men were waiting for them at a large door made of glass.

Chia thought the white furniture, white floor, white ceiling, and white feeling of emptiness and isolation made it a lonely, cold place to live. It had been small when she lived here, but cozy and colorful.

"How did you do this to the house?" Chia crossed her arms, almost suffocating Pip in the process. He quacked loudly and jumped down.

Viola straightened out her red dress and flicked her long brown hair, puckering her lips and watching her own reflection in the glass rather than looking at Chia. "Isn't it gorgeous? Mother, I mean Priscilla, upgraded it a little while ago."

"You can't trust her! She's leading us into a trap!" Jeremy had his arms up in fists and was jumping around like a boxing kangaroo protecting its young.

Viola's men all laughed at him. Viola did too.

Chia felt anger swelling in her stomach. She picked the fox up, surprised she was defending him after all his rudeness.

"Stop that. Jeremy is just worried about me. Aren't you, little one?"

"If one more person calls me little today, I will clobber them." Jeremy squirmed his way free of Chia's embrace, landing on his head instead of on his feet inside one of the pot plants. The soldiers laughed at him even harder.

"Sh. Settle down, everyone. We don't want to get caught and placed in the dungeons for real, now do we?" Viola picked up the small fox and turned him the right way up. "There you go. I think pink really is your color. You're most brave and becoming for a fox. You look more like a valiant knight."

Jeremy raised one eyebrow at her, then the other, before turning his back to her.

"What is the plan, Viola?" said Ms. Roberta.

"You will all wait here, and Chia and I will go inside to Priscilla's room. It will be far too conspicuous otherwise, trying to sneak past the ballroom. And besides, there is plenty of royalty attending, and we don't want them seeing you lot."

"I don't like the idea of us waiting here. What did we come for if not to help Chia?" Ms. Roberta was twisting the gold tassels on her dress so tightly, Chia was nervous they would snap in half.

"You came for moral support. We'll be back in a jiffy.

Men, you may go back to your normal posts, and tell no one of this."

"Are you sure, miss?" One of the soldiers finally spoke, his voice deep and mechanical sounding.

"Yes, yes. Off you go. Don't question me again, or I'll turn you off."

The men all turned toward the courtyard and marched away, out of sight, into the gardens. Viola turned to Chia. "You do trust me?" Her face drooped like Pip's did when he was looking sad and wanted a hug.

"Yes, I do." Chia gave everyone else a look of "not a word."

"Well, I'm not staying behind, no how, no way," said Pip.

"Me neither. Wherever he goes, I go," said Jeremy.

Pip looked astounded and speechless for the first time since he had talked.

Chia decided Pip and Jeremy were small enough to not been seen. Though Jeremy's hot pink fur was bright among all the white, she looked at the cross and determined look on his face and decided she didn't want to argue with him.

Ms. Roberta, on the other hand, would be impossible to hide.

"Ms. Roberta, can you stand here and pretend you're a statue?" Chia asked.

Ms. Roberta crossed her arms. "Are you sure it's what you want me to do? I'm much better protection for you if I come."

"We won't be long, and you can keep guard in case anything goes wrong."

Ms. Roberta tightened her arms more tightly together and looked at Viola. "All right. And, Chia . . ."

"Yes?"

"Please use your bow and arrow if at any moment you doubt Viola. That's what it's there for."

"I will," said Chia. But she wouldn't need it. Viola was good. She was sure. It was Priscilla who was the bad one. Together they would take her heart and be free of her once and for all. She looked Ms. Roberta in the eyes, gave her a quick hug, and followed Viola in through the glass doors.

Freedom was waiting for her.

11

PRISCILLA

This was it. Chia was about to enter the castle and come face-to-face with her stepmother, Priscilla. She wasn't feeling at all brave. Her legs were shaking uncontrollably. What if other soldiers caught them and she failed? Or worse still, what if the magic Clariel gave her didn't work?

"This will be easy, right?" she asked, sharing her fears with the others, hoping they'd make her feel better.

Viola reached for a door handle, "It will be easier than easy. You can only succeed with me by your side. Now follow me and be quiet." She opened the glass doors.

"Yeah, I feel better with *you* by my side," huffed Jeremy, rolling his eyes.

Chia walked inside what looked like a giant freezer, or the ice queen's evil palace. She tried to walk quietly, but her rain boots made a squeaking noise on the polished glass floor. Viola put her finger to her lips and glared at her. Chia shrugged her shoulders. She couldn't do much about it. But when she made even louder noises, Viola opened her palms and shook her head so hard, Chia decided it was best if she took off her boots.

She popped them next to the formal living room and noticed a painting on the wall. It was a portrait of her father. His green eyes seemed so alive to her. Like they were following her, urging her on. He was sitting in a brown chair. She didn't remember him having a brown chair like this. And he'd never posed for a painting that she could remember. He had an expression of pain on his face. Or was it fear? She looked closer.

"I wish you were here to tell me what to do," she said to the painting. She gently touched her father's face. Her mind was playing tricks on her. It looked like he was happier now. She could see happiness and hope dancing in his eyes. "I'm sorry I let you down. I'm so sorry you're dead."

Chia stepped back, gasping. She shook her head. For a moment, she thought her father's lips moved in the painting. But that wasn't possible.

"What are you doing? Talking to ghosts. Come on!" Viola kicked her red rain boots aside, grabbed Chia's arm, and pulled her away from the painting. Chia pushed her imagination and the pain of missing her father away. The painting wasn't moving or changing. She was making it up. She had to be. Just as Viola was dragging her around the corner, she took one last look. Her father stared back at her, glassy eyed.

They crept through the hallway, no other soldiers

anywhere. Voices and music danced toward them from the ballroom. Sweet and savory smells all intertwined through the air as they drew nearer the Christmas party. The music was melodic and magnetic, making Chia crave to dance. She hadn't danced for such a long time, she had probably forgotten how.

Viola put her forefinger to her lips, walking more slowly toward the entrance to the ball. Chia stifled her shock, her hand covering her mouth, as Viola unexpectedly grabbed Jeremy and Pip in one swoop and stuck them under her many layered dress. She casually waltzed past the open doorway of the ballroom and motioned with her hand for Chia to follow.

But Chia wasn't wearing a fancy dress like Viola's. She was dressed in her green jumpsuit and didn't even have shoes on. Her old socks, dirty and filled with small holes, were still on her feet.

She followed Viola's lead and tried as best as she could to saunter past the ballroom like a lady. It was especially hard for her not to giggle as Viola's dress violently puffed out in places. She guessed Pip and Jeremy were trying to escape the layers of material.

Just as Chia was almost past the doorway, she gave in to her curiosity and snuck a peek into the ballroom. What a ballroom it was! It was enormous. It made the Haven Room back at 66 Lilly Pilly Lane look tiny. Artemis would fit into this room and look small in comparison.

The ballroom was packed full of people, many of whom were dancing or feasting, while others talked and laughed together like they hadn't a care in the world. Counts, countesses, dukes, duchesses, kings, and queens seemed to make up the guests, Chia guessed. Most of them all wearing crowns of differing sizes.

She froze in place, her mouth open in awe and over-whelm. How did Priscilla even know all these people? Why would they come to her party of all people? She snapped out of her trance, as Viola pulled her back into motion.

"Sorry, I just, well . . . the people . . . the party."

"Shh. Yes, yes, but you're not here for that. You can't go in there with all those important people. Look at your-self," Viola whispered with agitation in her voice.

She was right, thought Chia, looking at herself and then at Viola, who stood with such grace and poise. She could never be like her.

As they reached yet more stairs, Jeremy and Pip burst forth from under Viola's dress.

"I never want to repeat what I saw under there. That is no place for a gentleman to be." Pip waddled out as if he were half dazed. Chia smiled at his ordeal, glad he had come with her. She felt comforted by his presence, but it didn't help her trembling fear, which was now working its way up her legs and spine and into her shoulders.

"You savage little moron!" yelled Jeremy, running circles around Viola in a rage.

"Is he always this ridiculous?" Viola lifted her chin high in the air.

"Do you know who I am? And you thrust me up your

dress like I'm a common garden fox? Why, I'm important! Just you wait."

Jeremy, dizzy from running around in circles so many times, sat down on Pip. "Oh yes, that's much better. Much better."

Pip's eyes bulged, and his bill opened as if ready to complain. Instead, he lay down and let Jeremy use him as a cushion.

Two soldiers ran down the stairs, long spears pointed toward them.

"Guards, I order you to let us pass. This is my sister and her two pets, and we are visiting Mother." Viola shook out her long hair and blew on her nails without so much as glancing at the guards.

They both nodded without speaking and walked away, just like that. Wow. Viola really was impressive with her power.

The carefully crafted glass stairs curled upward and seemed to go on forever as if they led to a high tower rather than another level of the castle.

Chia thought about facing Priscilla, her jaw now shaking like the rest of her. Her teeth clanged together violently. She was terrified, despite her sister and animal friends being by her side.

She had never seen what Priscilla looked like. And in this moment she was glad. But now she could see. Priscilla's commands were bad enough, but to see her would be beyond terrifying.

The heart in her pocket beat faster, in rhythm with her

own heart. Would she really be able to remove Priscilla's heart and replace it with this one?

"You should consider getting an elevator in this place," said Jeremy. "Or a secret hallway or something. This is killing my thighs." He panted his way up the stairs like an old man rather than a nimble fox.

"I'm sure this is doing wonders for my behind, and Heidi will appreciate me returning home to her fit and trim," said Pip.

"Bother!" Jeremy rolled his eyes and kept panting his way up the stairs. He made fox fists at Viola every time she looked at him.

Finally, at the top of the staircase, after what seemed like an eternity, there was another long hallway. It was longer than the hallway at 66 Lilly Pilly Lane, but not nearly as pretty. Here the walls were black, giving the upstairs area the feel of fear, depression, and anxiety. Viola led them to a large door at the end of the hall. It was painted sea blue and glistened like magic.

"This is Moth—I mean Priscilla's room. Duck and Fox, you stay here. Chia and I will do this."

Chia picked up Pip. "He has to come with me. He's my best friend."

"What am I? Pink fluff?" Jeremy growled like a tiger.

"No, Chia. I don't want your duck or fox friends to get injured. She could hurt them. Could you live with yourself if that happened?" Viola flicked her long hair and shook her finger at Chia. "Do you have the new heart?"

"Yes, I have it here. And I need to use a powder to get her real heart."

Chia didn't want to upset her sister, so she did as she said. She placed Pip down and reached into her pocket. She pulled out both bottles and the paper bag with the beating heart. The heart beat even faster as she held it in her hand, her own heart following suit.

"Give me the bottle and you keep the heart. You can trust me. I promise."

Chia looked down at Pip and Jeremy, who were both waving frantically at her and mouthing "No!"

She turned her back to them. "I trust you. You've only ever been kind to me. This is the bottle," she said, handing it to Viola. "Just sprinkle it on her. Then I'll be able to place my hand into her chest and take out her heart."

"What's the other bottle for?" asked Viola.

Chia looked down at her holey socks. "Nothing. It's just a spare. In case we needed more." She shoved it back into her pocket, holding her breath and counting in her mind. *One. Two. Three.* It was the only thing that ever helped her relax, and she was trembling so fiercely now, she almost dropped the heart.

Viola turned the door handle. "Mother? I came to check on you."

Four. Five. Six, Chia counted.

"I've brought someone to see you."

Seven. Eight. Nine.

"Is that you, Viola, my darling precious girl? Where have you been?"

Chia shuddered at the sweet melancholy of her stepmother's voice. *Ten. Eleven. Twelve.*

"Yes, Mother, it's me. And I have Chia with me. She's

come to visit you on Christmas. Then she'll return to the mines. She's been finding lots of diamonds for you." Viola's voice pranced in the air like a ballerina dancing on broken glass.

"Why did you bring the wretch back here?"

Chia breathed out, taking in a lungful of air. She turned to run, but Viola grabbed her arm and pulled her along, slamming the door in Jeremy's and Pip's faces.

Chia looked at the ground. She didn't want to look Priscilla in the eyes. She didn't want to see her hatred. She didn't want to make the fear in her heart spread throughout her whole body. Shaking, she felt like a frightened lamb about to be eaten by the Big Bad Wolf.

"She just wants to thank you for not sending her away or having her killed. She's very grateful you put her to work in the mines. Aren't you, Chia?" Viola walked around the large bed Priscilla lay on and fluffed the pillows thrown about on it.

Chia dared to glance around the room. It was decorated with so many diamonds she thought she must be at a royal palace. Diamonds she was made to dig up in the mines!

"Are you really grateful to me, Chia? Even though I killed your father?" Priscilla's voice shrilled like a rusty wheel on a bike. "Look at me when I speak to you!"

Chia willed herself to walk toward her, nice and close. Close enough to take her heart. She calmed her trembling hands, steadied her wobbling head, and looked Priscilla straight in the eyes.

"You can see me?"

"Yes. I can."

"How?"

Chia didn't want to tell her the truth. "I don't know. It just happened."

Priscilla's face was caked with heavy makeup. Her bright red cheeks and matching lips looked like a toddler had drawn them on for her. Her blue eye shadow hung on her lids like icing on a cake, thick and gooey. Her long thin nose looked out of place on her face. Her gray eyes, like dirty water, were limp and lifeless. "I don't believe you."

Chia thought she was foul enough when she had only heard Priscilla's voice. Now able to see, the woman before her was withered and worn out with wickedness. "I don't care what you believe! You're a nasty, evil, horrid woman, and . . ." Chia trembled with so much surprise rage she thought she might blow sky high.

She looked at Viola, who seemed shocked by Chia's comments, her mouth open and her cheeks bright red. But she didn't care. This was the moment. "Do it now. Sprinkle the powder," she commanded Viola.

Viola hesitated for a moment, her eyes glowing like glass. She moved slowly, like she may not do it at all, but then she pulled the lid off and threw the powder on Priscilla's chest.

"What are you doing? What is that?" Priscilla coughed uncontrollably, overcome by the magic powder that surrounded her.

"Take it, Chia. Do it!" Viola's command rang in her ears.

Chia closed her eyes, feeling safer in her darkness. She reached her left hand forward, her right hand still clutching the bag with the replacement heart. She held her breath and plunged her fist into Priscilla's chest. It felt cold. Icy cold. Dangerously cold. Her fingers slipped around Priscilla's rotten beating heart, finally grabbing on. She pulled with the force only hatred could muster. She pulled hard. She pulled fast.

Then she breathed out, relief mixed with fear, opened her eyes, and saw a bright red heart in her hands. Priscilla's heart. It didn't look like a human heart ought to look. It looked touched by magic. It was rosy red, almost plastic-like, and it glowed with mystical power.

"You did it. Quickly, the other heart. Priscilla's passed out, but we don't want to kill her." Viola looked calm and serene despite the desperation in her voice.

Chia's head was spinning and shaking and spinning some more. She bit down hard on her bottom lip, trying to distract herself with her own pain. It didn't work.

She put Priscilla's heart down on the bed, fumbling to get the other heart out of the bag. The replacement heart was brown and rusty-looking. It looked more mechanical than human.

She closed her eyes again and shoved her hand back into the unconscious Priscilla. Letting go of the heart in her chest cavity, Chia pulled her hand back out.

It was done.

She had done it.

Now she and Viola could be free of Priscilla forever.

Chia opened her eyes and heaved in gulps of air like a thirsty rat. She could feel her feet again. Her hands. Her body. But she was still shaking.

Priscilla stirred.

"Let's go!" Viola was at the door, holding Priscilla's beating heart. Her face was glowing with glee and giddiness, like she'd just come first at a race.

Just as Chia was about to flee, a cold hard hand took hold of Chia's wrist.

It was Priscilla.

Chia screamed.

Priscilla opened her eyes and bore into Chia's. "You think you've won, but you haven't. I will get back what is mine and more!"

Chia tried to pull away but couldn't. She looked at Viola, who was too busy looking at the heart she held triumphantly in her hand. Chia tried to call out but no words came to her.

She looked at Priscilla. This woman had taken everything from her.

Priscilla moved her other hand toward Chia's chest. Was she about to take her heart?

Chia stiffened, so full of fear she felt like a rabbit about to be made into stew. She remembered her father finding the courage to save a little rabbit in the forest one time. He had stopped a hunter from shooting it.

He had the courage she needed now. She thought of his love for animals. His love for her. Her friends needed her. Viola needed her. She remembered Artemis's words when he had given her his paper bark. *"It gives you courage."*

Chia pulled the piece of paper bark from her pocket with her free hand, threw it on Priscilla, and announced, "Lemon meringue pie, please!"

Priscilla released her hold, pie smothered all over her face. Her muffled yell and Viola's laughter were all Chia heard as she ran from the room, relieved she was finally away from Priscilla.

Chia ran faster than she knew she could. Guilt following beside her. She wasn't sure she had done the right thing, but it was done now, and there was no turning back. She ran past Viola, swept up Pip and Jeremy in one scoop, and ran down the stairs. She skipped the last few steps, tossing Jeremy and Pip into the air.

Ms. Roberta caught Pip first, then Jeremy. "Did you get it?" She looked triumphantly at a slew of soldiers at her feet.

Chia was so pleased to see her. "What happened? Why are you here?"

"I got bored in the garden, and besides, the music called to me." She danced a few steps and kicked a soldier who was coming to in the back, knocking him unconscious again.

"Roberta! What did you do to the men?" said Jeremy.

"It serves them right. They're not human, you know. They're robots. I just swapped a few wires when they tried to hold me back is all. And look at this." Ms. Roberta smiled, her perfect set of gold teeth gleaming to match the dangerously large emerald ring on her left hand. A ring Chia didn't remember seeing on her before.

"Where did you get that?" said Jeremy.

"I was just proposed to by a king. Yes, I was." She swayed from side to side, looking very pleased with herself.

Before anyone could say anything, Viola came down the stairs.

"I've got the heart—let's go. Did you do that?" she said, looking at the soldiers all around Ms. Roberta.

"Yes, I did," said Ms. Roberta, blowing on her ring while simultaneously putting Jeremy and Pip on the ground.

Before they could argue, Viola stuffed them back up her dress and casually sauntered past the open doors of the ballroom, looking straight ahead. Ms. Roberta followed behind her and waved to a tall and handsome young man with a long mustache that hung down past his chin on either side. His golden hair matched his rather large golden crown. He blew a kiss toward Ms. Roberta, and she pretended to catch it and put it in her pocket.

Chia half smiled, half waved, wondering how the king didn't seem at all concerned with the fact that Ms. Roberta was a statue. She pushed Ms. Roberta along, and shook her head at the king, who ignored her, his eyes only on Ms. Roberta.

They moved silently back toward the dungeons. No soldiers bothered to stop them this time. Several walked past, but Viola ordered them all away. As they approached

Artemis, Ms. Roberta patted Chia's arm, concern in her eyes. "Are you all right?"

"Yes, I'm fine," she lied. A strange tightness from her chest moved all the way down into her stomach and settled there. They had taken Priscilla's heart. And Priscilla had deserved it. Hadn't she?

12

ESCAPE

The deed was done. They had taken Priscilla's heart. Chia would present the heart to Clariel, and she and Viola could leave it all behind them and move on with their lives.

Chia was relieved to be back in the tunnel, safely on Matilda's back. But she still couldn't relax, the thought of Priscilla's last words ringing in her mind.

"Viola?"

"Yes?" Viola puffed up her red dress, getting the material in Jeremy's unhappy face.

"Why does everyone think you're bad when you're not?"

"Yeah, tell her, Viola. Tell the truth for once." Jeremy pummeled her red dress with both paws.

Viola ignored him. "You know me. You've known me all your life. It's true I'm conceited but not unkind, right?"

"Right," said Chia. She looked at Jeremy and Ms. Roberta. They looked forlorn and sad, rather than happy.

Everything had gone splendidly, yet they didn't look the slightest bit pleased.

"You did good, Chia. Now we can live somewhere quiet and peaceful. Right?" said Pip.

"Definitely. As soon as we arrive back, we'll hand over the heart and leave straight away." Chia felt relieved that none of her friends were hurt.

"Leave? Why will we leave? I want to see the house. Tell me more about it. Can't we stay there a while?" said Viola.

Chia felt happy to have her sister back. So, so happy. "It's very magical. It has a waterfall and a lake on the ceiling. And there are lilly pilly trees inside and toadstools and teepees. And there's a hallway, that always leads somewhere different every time. And even though you can go upstairs, you don't take stairs to get there. Just the same hallway. And mirrors. Yes, magical mirrors you walk through because there are no doors."

"Yep, that's it, tell her everything, why don't you." Jeremy scowled. "Lead the enemy right into our lair and give away our secrets. Keep going, don't let me stop you. Artemis has a plan. Yep. Uh-huh! Genius he is for letting you in."

Chia ignored him.

"What was it like living with Priscilla? Was she at least kind to you?"

"She wasn't unkind." Viola puckered her lips. "She thought of me as her daughter. But it was painful to endure. All the dances she made me go to. All the shopping she forced me to do. All the rich people she made me spend time with." Viola placed the back of her hand to her forehead, like she'd just been tortured.

"And I thought I was dramatic!" Pip yawned as if he was watching the most boring show in the world.

"Oh, brother!" chimed in Jeremy.

"What a marvelous pink fox you are. I've always wanted a pink fox fur hat." Viola reached out for Jeremy, who screamed in a shrill voice and jumped on top of Pip, who was still in Chia's arms.

"There, there, you two. Viola doesn't mean what she says. Ride on Artemis for a while. Ms. Roberta can look after you both." She flung them forward through the air toward Artemis, who walked rather slowly and heavily with Ms. Roberta on foot beside him. They were in deep conversation, but she couldn't make out what they were saying.

"Doesn't this monstrous spider go any faster? If I'd known how slow he was, we could have traveled by leopards," said Viola.

"Leopards?" Chia wondered where on earth Viola would find one.

"Yes. Mother, I mean Priscilla, just bought me two leopards for Christmas. I was dying to try them out. Apparently they're wonderful for riding on."

"Wow, you have suffered," said Chia.

"Thank you for recognizing my pain. You are a good sister. Ms. Roberta told me she was the one that rescued you. Is that true? I wonder why she would have bothered. I love you dearly, but there is nothing special about you. Not really."

Chia chewed her fingernails. Viola was right. There was nothing special about her at all. Why had Ms. Roberta bothered to rescue her? "I'm sure it was to send me to get Priscilla's heart."

"Yes, I suppose so. But why didn't she come to rescue me? I'm a far better choice to get Priscilla's heart."

"Yes, you are. You're right," said Chia.

"So can we stay a few days at Lilly Pilly Lane? Please say we can? I want to try swimming in the magical lake. And eating as much ice cream as I can tolerate. Mother only allows me three servings a day. Please say we can."

"Sure we can." Chia didn't want to let her sister down. Especially not after how she had helped her. She lay down, exhausted, and drifted into a deep sleep.

Chia woke up startled from a bad dream. Pip had morphed into Priscilla and was about to turn her into a diamond. She scrubbed her face with both hands, rubbing the dream away as the end of the tunnel shone the welcome light of 66 Lilly Pilly Lane into her eyes.

She rested her head back on Matilda, smiling to herself. Everything had gone so well. It had practically been easy. Too easy, even. Her new friends were all safe, she had rescued her sister, and they had taken Priscilla's heart.

Christmas music welcomed the spider and her riders back into the Haven room. Artemis and Ms. Roberta already looked at home in the foliage of the lilly pilly trees all around them. And the lake on the ceiling reflected little prisms of color all around the room, making it look even more magical than before.

Chia thought it seemed rather like the house was giving them its approval. As if it knew they had defeated Priscilla, and the heart was safe and sound back in the house. She had been so busy thinking about how she would save Viola and get Priscilla's heart, she had given little thought to what Clariel even wanted the heart *for*.

Chia climbed down from Matilda last and watched in awe as Ms. Roberta sprinkled the spider with dust. She shrank back to her normal size and scampered away under the brush of foliage, probably relieved to be free.

"How is the dust so magical?" asked Chia.

Ms. Roberta smiled. "Clariel makes it for us. It's all that's keeping us alive. Otherwise we would be . . ."

"Yes?" said Chia, keen to know more.

"Never mind. I'll see you later. I need to go see Robert." She skipped out the front door, leaving mystery and unanswered questions behind as always.

Viola pulled three pieces of bark from Artemis without asking.

"Ask for any food you want and it will give it to you," said Artemis not seeming to mind.

Viola nodded her head and trod off into the garden. Chia watched as she made a feast suitable for ten people rather than one. And enough ice cream to last a year.

Jeremy went for a nap in a teepee, and Pip went through the mirror in search of Heidi.

Chia stood in the garden, alone with Artemis.

Snowflakes fell all around her now, making it feel even more like Christmas. She looked up at the waterfall, which was frozen solid.

Magic was so hard to get used to. It seemed unpredictable and rather emotional. Artemis looked tired. His big blue eyes looked darker than usual, and the spot where his cheeks normally glowed a soft peach color looked dark and withered. His mouth equally sagged.

Chia wrapped her arms around his trunk. "You're not happy? We got Priscilla's heart. Clariel will be pleased. She will let Viola stay, and then help us go far, far away from Priscilla. Right?" Chia wanted him to say yes, yes, yes to all she had asked. He had to. This day was done. She had won. They all had.

Instead, Artemis closed his eyes and let out a big breath of unhappy air. "Are you happy, Chia? Really happy?"

She released her grip on him and sprung back in surprise. "What does my happiness have to do with anything?"

Artemis dropped some of his leaves and posies. They mixed with the snow and tickled Chia's nose as they gently landed on her face. She waved them away. She waved her own desires away at the same time. They didn't matter. Besides, she didn't even know what they were. All she had ever wanted was to help her father. And when he was gone, she had wanted to make him happy and save her sister. All that was done now.

"Happiness is the whole point of life," said Artemis.

Chia glanced at Viola in the distance, who was dancing around with a cream bun in one hand.

"I'm happy that my sister is happy. That's all I've ever wanted."

"Is it really all you've ever wanted?"

Annoyance tickled her nose and mind now. "Yes. Yes, it is. I know you may not understand that, but I promised my father I would look after her. That I would take care of her. So yes, it is all that matters." Chia blinked her blurred vision away. Tears gently rolled down her cheeks.

"I don't think this would make your father happy at all. I don't think your father intended for Viola to have everything she wanted and for you to suffer."

Chia felt a familiar frustration rush up into her chest. "I am not suffering. I am thrilled."

"Are you really?"

Chia's heart fluttered repeatedly in her chest. "Yes, I am. If Viola is happy, I am happy."

"But is Viola truly happy? Why do you think she helped you?"

"Because I'm her sister and she . . ." Chia choked on her words. She wanted to yell at Artemis for questioning her and Viola. Why couldn't he be happy for her? Everything had turned out perfectly. Everyone else was content — why couldn't he be?

"Chia?"

Chia nodded in acknowledgment.

"Chia. It's up to you now. You will need to put yourself first above all else if you are to help us. If you are to help yourself."

"What are you saying? What do you mean?" He was always talking in riddles. Everything was done. There was nothing more to do. But she nodded, not even sure why she was pretending to agree with him. She could not and would not put herself first. She didn't know how. She didn't understand why that even mattered. Helping others counted most. Was he not happy she had helped him? She looked into his sorrowful eyes.

"Why are you sad, Artemis?"

"Because you failed."

Chia fell backward into the snow. She wanted to yell at him that he was wrong. They had succeeded, not failed. She wanted to throw something at him as her anger swelled into her arms and legs. Instead, she stomped her left foot into the snow, realizing she had forgotten her rain boots back at Priscilla's castle, her toes wet through.

She turned toward the magic mirror. She ran, her chest heaving with rage and sadness and pain. Tingling and relief swept over her as it allowed her to pass. She stormed down the hallway through the second wall. It too allowed her to pass. She was in darkness.

She knew she was with Clariel.

She bent over to catch her breath and calm her nerves. Her chest heaved so much it practically touched her chin. Her legs wobbled. She was tempted to turn around and run back out the way she came, but as the soft light of Clariel's shadow glowed on the hanging sheet, she stood still, locked to the ground.

"Did you bring the heart?" came Clariel's soft, lingering tones.

"Yes, we did." Viola's voice rang out from behind her startling Chia. She had followed her.

"Good. Place it on the ground beneath the sheet," said Clariel.

Chia took a step back, bringing her side by side with Viola. She motioned with her eyes for Viola to do as she was asked. She had a sudden desire to give Clariel the heart and leave this place with Viola straight away.

"I will not!" said Viola.

"What? You have to give it to her. She's granting our wish to be free. She will help us go far away from here. To be free of Priscilla." Chia clicked the joints of her fingers, the clicking noise echoing off the walls.

"You want your own wish, don't you, Viola?" Clariel's voice sounded calm and serene despite Viola's rebellion. "Name it and you shall have it."

Viola cleared her throat and stood up at least an inch taller. She stuck her chin toward the ceiling and said, "I want to be the queen, like it's my birthright."

Chia looked at her sister, sure she'd gone mad. A queen? What was this nonsense?

Clariel's voice was firm with a touch of iciness. "Fine. I will see what I can do, but only if you give me the heart."

Chia took another step back. What was happening? Clariel had agreed as if it had all made sense. Like she understood.

"Wait!" said Chia, pulling Viola back by her dress. But Viola pulled away with ease and placed the heart on the floor under the sheet.

"You must now turn your back. Both of you," ordered Clariel.

Chia did as she was told. Her stomach tied up in knots. Her mind racing. Her heart fluttering madly. She closed her eyes, the darkness her only security in a day of blur and confusion.

Silence echoed off the round walls. Then the most painful sound Chia had ever heard bounced through the room and into her veins. It sounded like a bevy of bees, then morphed into the screeches of barn owls all calling out at once. She covered her ears and fell to the ground, pain searing through her head.

Confusion, chaos, and calamity smothered her senses. She opened her eyes to complete darkness. The lights had gone out. She was spinning out of control, her senses shutting down. A sheet wrapped around her, consuming her. The sounds intensified and turned into shrills and shrieks that sounded like the dead were awakening. Like a cemetery of zombies were all descending on her, and her nightmares were coming alive.

"Chia! Chia, wake up."

Chia recognized Jeremy's voice. His paws gently slapped both her cheeks. She opened her eyes, but it was still dark. "I can't see. Turn on the lights."

"They *are* on. You're as blind as a bat lost in the city of Babylon." Jeremy stopped slapping her. She heard him puff out a long, frustrated mouthful of air.

"Where's Viola? What happened? It was all so fast, and Artemis said mean things, and Viola wants to be queen, and Clariel said yes, and then screaming. Please tell me what happened."

"Quack. Quack quack! Quack quack quack quack quack!"

"Pip? Is that you? Tell me you're all right? What's happened to him?" She sat up, reaching out with both hands. Pip scampered into her arms and stuck his head under her armpit, quacking furiously.

"Shush, you silly duck. I can't explain with you ducking all over the place. Be quiet," Jeremy ordered.

"Explain? Explain what? Please tell me what's happened." Chia was exhausted and confused.

"Viola took Clariel. And the heart. She's gone, and with it, all the powers of the house. She's taken everything. She tricked you . . . Just as I predicted."

Chia felt his words penetrate through her chest and into her heart, squeezing it tightly. Her mind felt numb. Her body lifeless. Viola had tricked her? Viola had taken the magic of the house?

"Why can't I see?"

"You're blind again. And he's just an ordinary duck."

"What? How? Everything was fine. I turned around as Clariel asked and . . ."

What had happened when she had turned around? She had closed her eyes. Viola gave Clariel the heart. She had to have. She was good. She had to have been.

"I knew we couldn't trust her. Oh, you and your precious sister. Convinced she was good. Well, she's won, and we've lost. It's all over. Back to the mines for you."

"Quack! Quack quack! Quack quack!" Pip pulled his head out of Chia's armpit, arguing with Jeremy, but Chia couldn't understand him anymore. Or perhaps he was agreeing with Jeremy for once. Perhaps he was agreeing that she had failed at helping her sister, and failed Clariel. But most of all, she had failed her new friends. Artemis must have known. That was why he had seemed sad. They all had, but she hadn't listened.

She opened her mouth to say "I'm sorry," but a muffled cry emerged.

Her dreams and desires had vanished in one small moment. In seconds. She had not only lost everything, she had cost her friends everything too. And worst of all, she had lost her sister.

13

A PROMISE

Chia used her sense of touch to guide her back into the Haven Room. That and Pip's loud quacking showed her the way. She felt no bubbles or tingles or lightness as she moved through the mirror this time, but she was relieved it let her pass. The mood was heavy and solemn. There was no music. No splashing noises of the waterfall cascading into the lake on the ceiling. No laughter or feeling of joy. The room was devoid of all life and emotion.

"What's happened to the house? Please tell me." Part of Chia wanted to know, but most of her didn't. Her imagination was thinking up the worst things.

"Everything's destroyed because of *you*," said Jeremy, the same nasty tone in his voice as when Chia had first met him.

"Quack, quack quack!"

"Get off me, you nutty duck. Chia, control your pest."

Chia scrunched her nose toward Jeremy's voice and

scooped Pip up. He resisted, feathers flying up into Chia's face and irritating her nose. She held tight and hugged him. "There, there. You're my best friend, not a pest at all. I know you're upset. It will be fine. Whatever has happened, we can fix it." Pip nuzzled his head in her armpit.

"Fix it?" Jeremy growled. "How will you fix the fact that Artemis is nothing more than a tree? Or that Ms. Roberta has frozen solid into a statue. And the house is . . ." he stopped, sniffles echoing off the walls. "It's just a house now."

Chia placed Pip on the floor. Could it be true? She felt the cold hard ground beneath her feet. She sprawled her hands and moved them in a circular motion, her palms yearning for the softness of earth. But there was no grass, no moss, no life. Just cement.

"Please take me to Artemis." She didn't expect Jeremy would help her. Not after all she had done. She reached her hands up and forward, trying to find him herself. Something soft curled its way around her ankle, surprising her. Jeremy's paw gently guided her leg to the left. Her hands found the wilted bark of Artemis's trunk. She followed it up to his face.

"Oh no. No! Not you, dear, dear Artemis. What have I done?" Tears spilled from her eyes.

Artemis had been her friend. He had believed in her. He had mentored her and guided her. He had allowed Viola to come with them despite his misgivings. Her fingertips curled away from the solid round carvings that were Artemis's eyes. Artemis's eyes. They were open. But unmoving.

Lifeless.

Chia's throat was dry. "And Ms. Roberta?"

"Yep! She'll at least be pleased she's a statue with a happy smile on her face." Jeremy sniffled, his voice in pain.

Chia thought her chest might break open like a riverbank and leak out all her pain. Ms. Roberta had turned into a proper statue? She felt in front of her, Jeremy guiding her again. Her hands were numb as they met with Ms. Roberta's hard face. It wasn't moving. It wasn't breathing. Her fingers traced her smile. Motionless.

Chia's chest heaved. Her tears free flowing now, she leaned over, dropped Pip to the ground, and scooped up Jeremy before he could resist. She held him tightly at the waist and shook him back and forth with enough force to knock him unconscious. But it didn't. Instead, he yowled like a fox whose tail was on fire.

"Tell me what happened! Why are you fine and not the others? Did you do this?" Chia, surprised by her own anger and strength, dropped the fox and fell to the ground. She curled into a ball and wished she could turn back time and change all this.

If she'd just stayed in the mines and never come at all, this would never have happened. She wanted someone to blame, but she knew this was really all her fault.

She could hear Jeremy gasping for air. Then hissing like he was a garden snake. His voice come toward her, snarling and spitting and snitching at her. "Me? *Me?* You think I did this? You think I would hurt my friends? Didn't I warn Artemis not to let you in? Yes, I did. And you know why? Because *you* did this. You! Not me. You did all this for your sister, who betrayed you. Who betrayed us all."

"Viola . . ." It was all Chia could say. She knew that Jeremy was right. She had trusted her sister, instead of listening to their warnings. Now her friends were paying the price for her bad choice. Not to mention Pip was quacking at her instead of talking. And her precious sight was gone again.

"Jeremy. I'm sorry. I really am. You're right. You're right." She wiped her wet face and looked in his direction. "But I can fix this. I can find Viola and make her give the heart back. She's good, I'm sure. Priscilla made her do it."

"*Pfft.* After everything she's done, you're still defending her? You still want to help her? You're mad. Crazy is what you are. Artemis was wrong to let you in. Well, he's gone now, so it's up to me. I won't make the same mistake he did."

"There must be a way to fix this. What's happened to the house? To the lake and the waterfall . . . the trees and the nature?"

"It's all gone. Everything is gone. Your rotten sister tricked you, and now we're doomed. Doomed for eternity. Nothing we can do about it. It's all gone forever." Jeremy sobbed louder than a baby left alone in the wilderness.

"This is all my fault." Chia lay down on the cold hard ground.

"Yes, it is. You're right there. This is totally your fault. Your sister was all that mattered to you!"

Chia didn't understand. Her sister had only ever been good. She wasn't capable of doing this. It *had* to be Priscilla. "She helped us steal Priscilla's heart."

"She duped you! That's what she did. She was all you could think about. Your precious Viola. She stole everything from you. From us! Yet you still defend her!"

Chia's mind raced like a horse running wild, scared and traumatized. She didn't know how not to put Viola first. Viola was all that mattered. The dark all around her that had once been comforting and peaceful was now filled with fear and panic and loss. She had lost her sister. She had lost her friends. She had lost everything.

"We have to get my sister. We must. She's good, I tell you!" She was yelling now. Her words came back to her like boomerangs, prickling her skin and her conscience.

"Listen here, I don't care if you're the princess, you've lost your mind if you think I will help you save your good-for-nothing sister. She's destroyed everything and you let her!" Jeremy's voice boomed off the ceiling louder than a thunderstorm.

Chia's brain felt like it had sprouted wings and was bouncing off the walls of her skull. Princess? Had Jeremy just referred to her as a princess? She swallowed her tears and softened her tone. "Please tell me. I'm ready to listen. Tell me the truth. Please?"

"I will not tell you anything if it means you go rushing after Viola."

Chia held her breath, preparing to count to ten and

calm herself, but as Pip quacked and hid under her armpit, she breathed back out at once. She needed to be braver than this. How else would she save her sister? How else would she save her friends?

"Jeremy. I promise I won't do anything without you. Whatever we do next, we'll do it together. You, me, and Pip."

"Quack quack quack," agreed her duck.

"Artemis would never forgive me for telling you. I'm not allowed. And I won't let you lead us into trouble again. I'm doing this *by myself.*"

"Jeremy!" a new voice announced. "What a dreadful thing to say to the princess. I demand you tell her everything!" The voice was grainy with a hint of twang.

Chia helped herself up, new air filling her lungs. "Who are you?"

"I am Robert. Ms. Roberta and I—"

"You're the person she rushes off to meet all the time." Chia reached out her hands, hoping to feel the stranger.

"What are you doing here, Robert? You know you can't come inside. It's impossible you're even in here." Jeremy was talking in riddles again.

"When the house lost its magic, it let me in. Look, I'm fine," said Robert.

Chia wished she could look too, but she couldn't. "Can you help us make everything right?" Perhaps there was a glimmer of hope.

"Did you use the potion on Viola?" said Robert. "Or your bow and arrow?"

Chia dropped her head. She hadn't. She had trusted

Viola. Even Ms. Roberta had advised her to use her red arrows just to be sure. But she hadn't.

"I see. Well, it's done now. It's time for a new plan of action. It's up to the three of us to save the day." Robert's voice was bright and uplifting, like he truly believed what had happened could be undone.

"Quack quack!"

"Correction, my fine friend. Four of us. Is that you, Heidi?"

"No, I haven't seen Heidi. I don't know what's happened to her," said Jeremy.

"Quack quack quack quack quack quack!"

Bang! Crash! It sounded like Pip was trying to fly into the mirror with no luck.

"We have to tell Chia the truth, or she won't help us," said Robert, his voice coming closer.

Chia heard the *cloppity clop* of what sounded like a horse's steps. "What are you?"

"Excuse me for not formally introducing myself. I'm a goat. I'm Ms. Roberta's brother. Like you and Viola. We're twins too." He paused as if waiting for the information to sink in. "So you see, I can certainly understand how important Viola is to you. I would never allow any harm come to my sister. And nor should you let any come to yours."

Chia decided on the spot that Robert was her favorite in the house. Next to Artemis. He sounded charming and kind and considerate. Like he understood her, or at least cared to try. "Thank you. So you understand why I have to go back and help her?"

"Go back? Oh, dear, no. You can't do that. If Priscilla has Clariel, she has magic far beyond what you know or understand. There is no way to defeat her. No, no, our only option now is to return to what's left of Faren."

"Faren?" Chia felt butterflies in her stomach as she said the word.

"Yes, Faren. The fairy kingdom. Where we all come from. Jeremy! Didn't you at least tell her that part?" Robert said with tones of disgust.

Chia couldn't find any thoughts floating about in her head. In fact it felt like her mind was totally empty. Fairy kingdom? This was getting silly. It wasn't possible.

Robert cleared his throat. Chia felt his soft hoof upon her open hand. "It's where you're really from. And your mother."

"Go ahead," yelled Jeremy. "Tell her everything and doom us all to this curse forever. Sure, why not. You're not in charge here, Robert. I am, and I order you to stop."

Chia's blood boiled.

All the rage she had been so good at pushing down began to rise in her like a silent volcano about to come alive. A force similar to hot lava moved its way up her stomach and into her mouth. She was sick of not being told the truth.

"Tell me everything, or I'll—I'll—I'll use my bow and arrow on you!" She pulled it off her back, placing an arrow in her bow and pointing it in the general direction of Jeremy. She couldn't be sure he was still there, but she intended to use it.

"Relax! Put that down." She could hear Jeremy

jumping from side to side. "You're so uptight. I would tell you, but Artemis said you need to figure it out yourself, otherwise the curse can't be broken. Don't you want Artemis and Ms. Roberta back? You're happy to help yourself, but not a care in the world about anyone other than your rotten sister."

"Your people need your help, Your Majesty," Robert added.

Chia's mind raced all around the room and back into her head. "I don't believe you. I can't believe you. It's not possible. You're all liars." She pulled back her bow and flung an arrow through the air, not bothering to direct her thoughts. She heard it bounce off something hard.

"Jeremy, I insist we tell her everything. Can't you see she's suffering? Forget the curse. Being a goat's not so bad. And you, a fox. Foxes are very important animals, you know."

Chia heard Jeremy grumble. Then breathe out heavily. "Tell her then. I won't stop you."

Chia released her clenched fists and relaxed her face. She would finally discover the truth.

14

THE TRUTH

Chia crumpled to the ground, relieved she would finally know everything. Who she really was. Who her mother really was. How she was connected to this place and to these creatures. "Tell me about the curse." Her mouth went suddenly dry, as if all life was draining out of her body.

"My sister did you a disservice not telling you anything at all," said Robert.

"Artemis forbade it, and you know why," said Jeremy.

"He's a regular tree now, so there's not much he can do to stop us. It's up to you and me. We have to get Chia back to Faren, so she can do what she was born to from the beginning."

"What was I born to do?" All Chia knew to do was dig for diamonds in the mines.

"Lead!" yelled Robert. "You must lead. Only you can lead us to a new beginning."

Chia's legs shook, and her heart broke. What about

her sister? "I won't do anything before rescuing my sister from Priscilla."

"Viola has betrayed you. Again." Robert spoke softly despite his cutting words. "She's on Priscilla's side now. For good."

"*Humph!* Forget it, she will not stop trying to save her sister. We're doomed. All of us. I'm doomed to be a fox forever!"

Chia dug her fingers into the bow. "Why are you still a fox? Everyone else has lost their magic, so why haven't you? Tell me why you're still fine."

"Fine? Fine! You think me turning into a brown fox is *fine*, do you? Being a fox in the first place is bad enough, but at least when I was pink, I had some pizzazz. Now I'm just a boring brown fox."

"*Quack quack!*" Pip seemed to agree with him.

Jeremy snarled at Pip. "Be quiet! I can still eat you! In fact, you're pretty much all there is to eat now."

"*Quack quack quack quack QUACK!*" Pip jumped onto Chia's lap.

"We can find Viola, and I promise I will use the bottle and the bow and arrow! I'll do it right this time. Please let me. Help me get there. I can't see. I need your help."

"Viola took your eyes twice, and you still want to help her?" said Robert.

"What?" Chia didn't understand. What was Robert talking about?

"Dear fellow, you told her about her eyesight at least? *Tut tut tut!*" Robert finished his sentence with a meaw.

"My eyesight?" Chia felt faint with each new piece of information.

Robert cleared his throat. "You *are* the daughter of the queen. The queen of the fairies. You are the firstborn and heir to the throne. Tell her, Jeremy."

"It's true," mumbled Jeremy.

Chia's mind chewed on the information the way she used to chew on the hard pieces of bread she ate for dinner in the mine. She wanted to reject this nonsense. To run back home to Viola. Even the mines felt tempting to her right now. A fairy princess? Air to the throne of *fairies*? Her? It wasn't possible.

"What's Priscilla got to do with any of this?" she asked.

Robert cleared his throat. "Priscilla stole your mother's heart."

"You're telling her absolutely everything?" said Jeremy, panting hysterically.

"Yes, everything. It's the only way," said Robert.

"Go on, please?" Chia was desperate to know more.

"Your mother married a mortal man, George Gregola. It was forbidden, but she did it nonetheless, and lived with your father on—"

"Lavender Hill," said Chia. Was it possible this was true?

"Yes, indeedy. That's exactly where they lived. Artemis, Ms. Roberta, Heidi, and Jeremy were her royal army. They were the only ones that went with her. To protect her."

Chia's feet felt limp. It sounded like something out of a fairy tale. "You're all fairies then?"

"I am," said Robert. "And so is my sister, and Heidi.

Jeremy here, fine old man, is a goblin prince. And Artemis, an elf prince. How they came to serve your mother is another story."

"Jeremy is really a goblin? That explains a lot!" said Chia, thinking Jeremy had behaved like a goblin the whole time.

"Grff!" Jeremy replied.

Robert stomped one of his four feet and mewed loudly. "Let me continue. This is your story. Your heritage. Priscilla was your mother's maid. She is nothing but an ordinary mortal. We believe she snuck into your mother's room in the middle of the night and stole her heart."

"When? How old was I?" Chia was trying hard to sort all the pieces together.

"You were ten. It has been two years now," said Robert.

Chia's stomach churned and tousled with nausea. "But that's not possible. My mother died when I was born, not when I was ten. My father raised me and Viola. You must have the wrong girl. I'm not a fairy. I can't be. This is silly."

"You are the most stubborn person I've ever met!" said Jeremy.

"Quack quack!" Pip argued back.

"Chia, you have also been living in the curse. It has altered your memories. I'm telling you the truth. I swear it on your mother's honor. Your mother and father both raised you, together. And Chia, this is the bit you need to know most of all." Robert paused and made a strained mewing noise.

"Go on then," said Chia, fighting her own mind whether or not to believe all this. It was all so far-fetched.

"*You were never blind.* When Priscilla stole your mother's heart, it was Viola who helped her do it. She is the blind one. She stole your eyesight, and your memories along with it."

Chia sat down on the ground. She felt empty. She felt alone. She felt betrayed. Yet despite all that she heard, she couldn't believe it. She wouldn't. None of it made sense. She remembered nothing. Her mother had died when she was born. She had to have. She was blind because of a fever she had as a child. And her father had raised her. Alone. Hadn't he? She shoved the tsunami of emotions threatening to overtake her deep into her stomach, keeping them there with a hard swallow.

"Open your mind. We're breaking all the rules and giving up our chance to ever turn back to our usual selves. Why would we lie to you now?" Jeremy sounded sincere.

Jeremy had never been kind to her, but he hadn't ever lied either. He had been right when he advised Artemis to throw her out. She had caused this. "And the curse?"

"For two years we've been stuck like this. For two years all my people have been nothing more than goats. And the royal guards have been trapped inside this house. Until . . ."

"Until what?" Chia wanted to know more than anything.

"Until you spoke up to Hitchens that day in the mines. It was the reason Roberta could come and help you. You stood up for yourself. You finally put yourself first."

Chia widened her eyes, thinking back to yesterday. Something unexpected had risen in her, and she had challenged Hitchens. She had never done that before, and soon after being punished for it, Ms. Roberta had turned up to rescue her.

"That was the beginning. You began to break the curse. It's the reason the others could suddenly leave the house. You're the key to everything. The curse was made by someone selfish— Priscilla. Only a person true of heart and self-loving can break it, Chia. That person is you! But you have to do it because you *want* to. Because you love us. Because you love yourself. You have to choose it for you. If you know the truth, the curse can never be broken. It's complicated, but it's the nature of curses. Otherwise we would have broken it ourselves." Robert exhaled, then sucked in a giant breath.

"She *could have* broken the curse, but now we've told her, she can't break the curse anymore, genius." Jeremy's curt, rancid voice was back to match his goblin disposition.

Chia's chest was empty. As if her heart had fallen right out of her body and washed away with all the rest of the magic. Her mind raced through all her memories. Memories with her and her father. Memories of her sister. She was nice. She always had been. But her memories weren't real. None of it was real! As the sickening feeling of truth surfed through her stomach, she collapsed onto the floor. No tears came this time. Only the sharp pain of loss.

"Now you understand why Artemis didn't want to tell you any of this. I warned you!" Jeremy's voice was cutting.

Robert rubbed himself against Chia's limp body. "It's a lot to take in, but you needed to hear the truth. I've been thinking. Maybe you're right. Perhaps we can still defeat Priscilla."

"How?" said Chia, hopeful this meant she could save her sister.

"Do you have the bottle of fairy dust you were meant to use on Viola?" Robert's voice danced around her with joy.

"I suppose. I don't know."

Chia heard rustling. Then silence. Then more rustling.

"It's hard without hands, but a-ha! We have fairy dust. Right from Clariel. We can do this! We might defeat Priscilla and turn back into our true selves after all," said Robert.

"What are you talking about? Make yourself clear. I can't stand it when you talk in circles," growled Jeremy.

"With this dust, we can make Chia forget again."

"Make me forget? Why would you do that?"

"If you forget, then you can still break the curse," said Robert.

"So, what was the point in telling her in the first place? Fairies seriously have beans for brains," said Jeremy.

"She's satisfied now. Some part of her might remember enough to do it right this time. I believe in you, Chia." Robert was positively glowing with excitement.

"But she won't. She'll just go back to wanting to save Viola. That's how daft she is."

"Viola really is good," said Chia.

"See what I mean?" said Jeremy. "She's convinced Viola's good. Chia, for the last time, when Priscilla took your mother's heart, and Viola went with her, they tricked you with fairy dust. All your memories of your father dying, and the need to save Viola, aren't true. Your father's alive and Viola was never good. Never. She took your eyesight. And before that, she was a spoiled little brat. Your mother sent her to Faren in the hope it would teach her compassion. But it only made her worse. She's an entitled, worthless little turd." Jeremy sounded pleased to be taunting Chia again.

"Sounds like someone else I know," said Robert.

Chia's mind raced. "My father's alive?"

"Yes, he is, probably kept prisoner somewhere by Priscilla. You can save him. You can save us all," pleaded Robert.

Light spread through Chia's body as if a million fairies had suddenly been brought back to life. She lifted her head toward Robert and reached out for his head, patting it gently. Her father might be alive. Everything she had believed was a lie. "How will I do it when I forget? I'll think Viola is good again and want only to save her."

"Finally, you're being reasonable. You see, she admits it." Jeremy clapped.

"You really can save your sister from her wicked ways," said Robert. "But you have to do it for yourself. Not for anyone else. You are the rightful queen. Only you can defeat Priscilla. It has to be *you*."

"*Pfft*. Sure. If you think Little Miss Stubborn here is

going to finally put herself first, you've got something else coming," said Jeremy.

"We shall see. Chia, what do you say?"

"I'll do it. If it might save all my friends, I'll do it."

"Hooray! Oh, I think there might be enough in here for you to see with too. Would you like your eyesight back?"

Chia was missing the light and colors immensely. She was about to say yes when she thought of Pip. "I think I would prefer that Pip could speak again, please."

"Pfft, Pfft, Pfft," spat Jeremy. "She still can't put herself first. Even now. She's hopeless. We've no chance. We'll be killed, roasted, and eaten by Priscilla herself!"

Chia ignored Jeremy. "Robert, is Clariel my mother?" She wasn't sure why she asked. Robert hadn't told her what had happened to her mother when Priscilla took her heart. Or if she was even still alive.

Robert cleared his throat and waited a long moment before speaking. "No. Clariel is a butterfly. She makes fairy dust from diamonds. Diamonds you were made to dig. The diamonds themselves have magic, but when Clariel turns them into fairy dust, they have immense power. Power that Priscilla now commands."

Chia gulped in the information. Fairies and fairy dust and butterflies and magic. It was overwhelming, and amazing, but her family mattered more than that. "What happened to my mother?"

"Go on then, tell her. She'll forget anyway," said Jeremy.

Chia was grateful he had agreed with something for

once. She clutched Pip to her a little more tightly. Her father was still alive. Maybe her mother too. She had never met her, according to her memories. What was she like? Was she happy and bright? Or serious and melancholy? Who was her mother?

"Chia, your mother is . . ." Robert stopped short.

"Yes?" Chia asked, tension creeping into her face. "Please tell me."

"Your mother is . . . Queen Lilly Pilly. Also known as 66 Lilly Pilly Lane."

15

6,958

Chia was speechless. The house was her mother? This whole time no one had told her. She thought back to the countless times they had referred to it as if it were a person. It *was* a person the whole time. And not just any person. It was her mother. And the queen of the fairies, no less. She felt silly not knowing. She knew that her mother's name was Lilly, but she'd never guessed this.

She closed her eyes, now understanding why she had felt at home here. She felt loved and cared for, safe and protected inside these four walls. But she had missed her chance to talk to the house. To speak with her mother. It lay all around her, an empty shell. Nothing more than a house. Dead. Lifeless.

"If we defeat Priscilla and get back my mother's heart, is there a chance we can save her?"

"Perhaps," said Robert.

Chia hung her head. She wanted to ask so many questions about her mother, and the curse, and where her father was. But she sensed it was pointless. She knew that all of it didn't matter unless she defeated Priscilla and got her mother's heart back. The stinging sensation in her own heart reminded her of how many times she'd been disappointed before. She couldn't allow it to happen again. She had to break the curse. Her mother, her sister, and her father depended on it. And her friends.

Chia had just discovered so much about who she was, and she was about to forget it all. She would return to knowing nothing. But now more than ever, she knew it was a risk she had to take.

She stood up, stretching herself to feel taller, and gulped hard, preparing for Robert to sprinkle her with fairy dust. Fairy dust that would make her forget who she really was. Who everyone really was.

"Robert?"

"Yes, Your Majesty?"

"Oh, stop calling her that, for goblin's sake!" Jeremy was as grumpy as ever.

"Do I have wings?" It was a silly question, and she had so many others, like where Faren, the fairy kingdom, was, and were fairies tiny, and how were they friends with elves and goblins, but somehow all she could think of was whether she could fly.

"Yes, of course you have wings. We all do. When we're fairies. And we're not little either. That's just a myth. Are you ready? I am about to sprinkle you with powder and you will forget. When you come to, I will agree to help save your sister. I'll see you on the other side."

"Hurry up already. I ain't getting any younger!" yelled Jeremy.

"Goodbye, my fair princess. I shall always be your royal subject."

Chia felt a slight tickling sensation start from the crown of her head and spread itself ever so softly all the way to her toes. She felt like she was being rocked to and fro, as if she lay in a bassinet, a baby again. All thoughts floated away. All desires drifted from her. A sweet lullaby filled her mind. She sang along to it in her head. It felt comforting and soothing.

"Chia!"

"Chia!"

"Chia, wake up!"

Chia sat up. She was on the ground. She was . . . What was she doing? "Pip, is that you?"

She remembered. Viola had taken Priscilla's heart and had stolen the magic of the house. Artemis was a tree, and Ms. Roberta a statue, frozen solid and no longer able to speak and move. And her eyesight was gone. She was blind once more.

"Yes, it's me. I'm so glad you're okay, but I really need to find Heidi."

"Pip, wait." She heard him waddle away. "Jeremy?" she called, hoping he was all right.

"Yep. Still here. Still annoyed. Still hungry for duck."

Chia felt somehow better knowing Jeremy was his old self.

A new voice startled her onto her feet. "Jeremy, do

introduce me to the child. We haven't had the pleasure of meeting yet."

Chia wondered who was speaking.

"Chia, Robert. Robert, Chia."

"*Tut tut,* you can do better than that. I am so pleased to make your acquaintance. I am Robert."

"Are you the same Robert that Ms. Roberta always ran away to meet?" said Chia.

"Yes, one and the same. Well done for remembering the *important* things. I'm Ms. Roberta's twin brother. I am here to help save your sister."

Chia had never felt more relieved. "Thank you. I know she took the heart, but I'm absolutely sure Priscilla made her do it. I know she did."

"Yep. Sure, whatever you say Maddie Mad Eye!" scowled Jeremy.

Chia felt annoyed with Jeremy, but she was getting better at ignoring him.

"I hope I don't offend you with the fact I am a goat, not a statue like my sister," said Robert.

Nothing much surprised Chia these days. "A goat? Well, that makes for interesting variety. And you're definitely going to help me save my sister?"

"Yes, together we shall save everyone. Right, Jeremy?"

"Yup! Whatever."

"I'm blind you know. I can't see. So you'll have to help me." How she longed to be able to see again. To fill her mind with images, and objects, and warm, happy faces smiling at her.

"Never mind that. I have an entire team at your disposal," said Robert. "And you have your bow and arrows, and we have a fierce and angry fox. We can do anything."

Chia loved how enthusiastic and encouraging Robert was. She liked him straight away. Almost as much as Artemis.

"Let us be off. We shall march to Priscilla's castle and defeat the evil witch at once." He sounded like an over-confident knight in shining armor.

"Wait for us. Come, my darling," said Pip.

Chia could hear quite a commotion of flapping feathers and quacking mayhem. What was happening?

"Haha! Now that's made my day. Your lunatic duck is dragging poor Heidi along like a prisoner. What's the matter, your love spell wearing off, is it? She hates you. No amount of magic will ever change that!" Jeremy sounded like he was thoroughly enjoying himself.

"Be quiet or I'll—I'll—use the Mind Weaver on you next," Pip threatened. "Heidi, what's happened to you? Heidi, it's me, the love of your life. Chia, help me. Help me!" Pip was hysterical.

"Ha! Your Mind Weaver won't work on me! I'm a—"

"Meow, meow!"

"Robert, have you lost your mind?" said Jeremy.

"*Ahem.* No, chap, I think you were about to say something you might regret," said Robert.

"Right."

Chia had no idea what they were talking about. They all sounded like they had gone mad. Perhaps this was a result of the heart being taken.

"Chia, please help Heidi," begged Pip.

Chia reached out her hands, but without her sight, she felt hopeless. She followed the noise and grabbed hold of a duck. Not sure which one, but she had one.

"Quack, quack, quack!"

Chia guessed she had picked up Heidi, who now seemed unable to talk. She too had been affected by the taking of Clariel. She was just an ordinary duck.

"Here, give Heidi to me," said Jeremy, taking the duck from her hands. "And you, nutty duck, stay away from her. Your Mind Weaver won't work on her twice. Save it for those we need to conquer."

"Come here, Pip," said Chia.

He jumped into her arms. "I love Heidi, and now she doesn't love me back," he whimpered. He snuggled his head in her armpit.

Chia cuddled him tight. He too had lost someone he loved. Her heart ached and spun and popped at her. It was time to get Viola. "What's the plan?"

"Follow me. I shall lead you to my troops. Together, we will get Clariel and the heart back, defeat Priscilla, and save your sister." Robert spoke like a true leader.

Chia was so glad he was here and willing to help her. She didn't think Jeremy would be pleased about it, but she didn't care. She had to do the right thing and rescue her sister, get the heart back, and help her friends.

It was quiet outside. Deafeningly quiet. Chia smelled the ocean breeze and listened gratefully for the calm lapping of the water. But her heart was determined to beat faster than a ticking time bomb.

"Don't you have any shoes?" said Robert.

"No. I forgot them at Priscilla's castle. I'm fine. I don't care."

"Nonsense, jump onto my back. We're about to go through mud, and Your Highn—I mean, your feet will get cold."

Chia heard a slapping sound.

"Was that really necessary, old chap?" said Robert.

"Just swatting at a fly," said Jeremy.

Chia scrunched up her nose, wondering why Jeremy and Robert were being so silly and petty at a time like this. Everything was at stake. They needed to focus.

She climbed onto Robert's back, glad for the rest, still clutching tightly to Pip. She felt Jeremy riding on Robert too, and Heidi snuggled in tightly in front of her.

"I never knew foxes were so lazy they couldn't walk," said Chia, glad to finally have a knock at Jeremy.

"Yes, I'm surprised you're riding on me today, Jeremy."

"If you tell anyone, and I mean anyone, I rode on your back, I'll make sure you're dinner! Got me?" Jeremy's voice was foul and filled with frustration.

"The ducks don't mind riding on me, so why do you care so much? Too much pride that hasn't been fixed by being a pink fox?" said Robert.

"Be quiet! I'm trying to concentrate." Jeremy made a loud huffing sound and said no more.

The strong wind became still. The soft hooves tromping in the mud stopped. The happy chirping of the birds vanished.

"Are we here?" whispered Chia.

"Shh. Listen," Robert whispered back to her.

Chia's hearing was as good as any rabbit or fox. Possibly better. But she couldn't hear a thing. She waited for what felt like several minutes. Still nothing moved or stirred.

"Well?"

"Shh!"

Just when she was about to yell she'd had enough of waiting, just as it felt like she'd been waiting for hours instead of minutes, she heard it. A soft buzzing sound. Like bees searching for honey, but different. It was more musical. More in tune. More melodic.

She wished she could see what the others could see. What was making that noise? Before she could ask questions, she heard the buzzing turn into singing. Words she didn't recognize filled the air. It was how she imagined singing angels would sound.

"What is that?" Chia's heart felt like it flipped as high and skillfully as a jumping frog. Chills ran up and down her spine. How she longed to see.

"Are you sure it's them?" said Jeremy, his voice as gruff as ever.

"Yes, it's them. I live with them, don't I?" said Robert.

"It could be a trap. She might have taken them, now that she can, and be about to catch us, kill us, and eat us!" Jeremy sounded frantic and frightened.

Chia was worried. What were they talking about? She couldn't make sense of anything they were saying.

Robert cleared his throat and mewed deeply. "We're not being tricked. It's them, I tell you. I'm sure."

Chia wanted to run away through the fields with her Pip and never return. But she stayed put. Her head heavy with what she knew she must do—go forward no matter what the risk.

"Yes, Robert. Go on. Lead us to your people." As she heard her words come back through her ears, she sounded different than normal. More calm. More confident. More courageous. But she didn't feel that way inside.

"How I hate goats!" yelled Jeremy over the singing, which now rang through the fields and was getting louder and louder.

"They're all goats?" said Chia. How would a herd of goats defeat Priscilla? They could sing her to sleep, she reasoned, almost dozing off herself. It was mesmerizing. Almost hypnotic. "Tell me what is around me. I can't see."

"Of course Your High—I mean, yes, high goats, lots of goats. They have sharp horns and will defeat Priscilla's army." Robert sounded confident in himself.

"How will goats defeat Priscilla?" Chia was yelling to be heard.

The singing stopped at once. As if on command.

"This is Chia, everyone. She's a regular girl, just a nobody, and we're going to help her. Understood?" Robert sounded tense and troubled. Chia wondered what was going on.

"Will she lift the curse?" yelled a new voice.

"Will she lead us?" called another.

"Your Majesty!" said a third.

What were they were talking about? She shook her head at the thought of not one, but an entire pack of talking goats. "What do they mean, Robert? Who are they talking to? Are you their king?"

"Yes, yes, I'm the king goat. Settle, my people, settle. No more speaking. Not a word, I command you. And no more singing. We shall march for the castle and slay Priscilla."

"We are to be freed," called a random goat.

"Hoorah," yelled many. And then many more.

Chia looked around as if she could see. She was bewildered. So many voices. Cheering and mewing and muttering her name. She felt a little bit of hope. A glimmer of possibility that together they might defeat Priscilla once and for all.

"But first we eat!" called Robert.

Eat? What was there to eat? There was no Artemis to create magic with his paper bark. No magic of 66 Lilly Pilly Lane to bring things to life. They were in an open field. Chia put her arms out, wondering why it had gone silent again. All that could be heard was the soft sound of chewing.

"Jeremy? Are you here?"

"Yeah. I'm here."

"What are we eating?"

"*We're* not eating. They are. Grass. Goats! It's all they think about. Eating."

"Please tell me how I'm supposed to believe that they will somehow help us."

"Not too smart, goats, but upset them and they can rip you to shreds. They'll be useful against Priscilla's army."

"You really think we can beat her and get Clariel back with a few goats? How many of them are there?"

"Six thousand, nice hundred, and fifty-eight on my last count."

Chia couldn't believe her ears. She was surrounded by 6,958 goats?

"Who is Clariel?" she asked suddenly. Her mouth had a mind of its own.

"I can't tell you that. Artemis made me promise not to tell you a thing."

"Can you at least tell me why you can't tell me anything?" Chia felt anger coursing up her chest like a snake.

"Because then you can't break the curse."

"I'm supposed to break a curse?"

"Yep. You got it. You're not even supposed to know about the curse. I'm a blabbermouth! Hopefully that won't ruin everything. Now stop asking questions."

Chia reached out her hands, guessing from the sound of his voice where Jeremy was. She grabbed him around the throat and lifted him clean off the ground. "Tell me who Clariel is! And who the heart belongs to." She put him down, loosening her grip slightly, but still holding on.

"Fine! Let me go! You savage. You've got a temper on you, don't you?"

"My temper is equal to yours," said Chia.

"Don't blame me if trying to break the curse doesn't work because I told you."

Chia caught hold of Pip with one hand as he waddled into her arms, the other hand ready to grip Jeremy more tightly if needed. "Go on. Tell me everything!"

"Clariel is an angel, and it's her heart," said Jeremy. He coughed uncontrollably.

Chia wasn't sure why, but something didn't feel right. None of it made sense. "Are you telling me the truth?"

"Of course I am. You asked and I told you. Touch me again and—I warn you—I bite."

"And why didn't Artemis want you to tell me that? I already knew that."

"Beats me. You have to want to do what you're doing or it won't work."

"What won't work?"

"Breaking the curse! Look, I'm not saying another word, and you can choke me all you like. Just focus on your rotten sister and leave the rest to me."

Chia squeezed her hand tighter around Jeremy's throat. "Tell me my sister is good. Admit it. Priscilla's controlling her. She has to be."

Jeremy choked and sputtered until Chia eased the pressure on his throat. "Viola's always been self-centered and greedy. She's not good. Now let me go."

Chia released her hand and heard Jeremy slide away. If Clariel was an angel, then what did Priscilla want with her? And why had Priscilla stolen her heart? She pulled her bow and arrows from her shoulder and thought of Priscilla. She would use them on her and get the truth.

She would force her to reveal everything. And to admit that it was her the whole time who had influenced Viola. Viola was good. Of this she was sure, and this time she would prove it to Jeremy.

And to herself.

16

THE FEATHER

Chia wasn't looking forward to confronting Priscilla again. Twice in two days was far too much of her stepmother. But this time would be the last time ever, and that made her happy. Never seeing Priscilla again kept her spirits high as they marched onward for the rest of the day.

"How many days did you say this would take?" Chia asked, feeling stiff from sitting on a goat for so many hours. Her stomach rumbled. But there was only grass all around them. And the goats traveled so slowly.

"If my calculations are correct, it will take us fifty-eight days, give or take a few," said Robert.

"Fifty-eight days? That's the silliest thing I've ever heard. Can't we use magic?" She wished Artemis was here to carry them to the castle nice and quickly, or Ms. Roberta to spin them there even faster. "What about the powder I didn't use on Viola? Can't we use that?"

No one answered her. Chia reached into her pocket and felt around for the bottles of magical dust. She whisked out both the bottles Clariel had given her, and the feather too. One bottle was empty. But the other would be full. She had not used the powder on Viola as Clariel had instructed. A point she now sorely regretted. But perhaps it was a blessing in disguise. "Here, I have more powder. Can this help?" She held up both bottles, wondering why both the bottles felt empty to her. Had someone else used the powder?

Robert began to cough violently, as if trying to change the subject. He almost knocked Chia off his back.

"Are you all right? I hope I'm not tiring you. I can walk. Really, I can."

"*Quack!* He's coughing because he—*mmmm, mmmm, mmmm.*" Pip was halfway through talking when Jeremy covered his bill. "Ouch! What did you do that for? Covering my mouth like I'm not supposed to . . . oh yeah, I'm not supposed to . . ."

"You're welcome. Now I'm covered in duck saliva. Disgusting!" Jeremy's conversation with Pip was making Chia wonder what was going on. Her friends were acting like they were keeping something from her. She reached out her hands, hoping she would get ahold of Jeremy again to squeeze the truth out of him.

"You're not getting anywhere near me, Chia, and if you make me tell you anything I'm not supposed to, I will seriously eat your duck. For real!"

"Whatever!" said Pip. "I don't believe you. And when Heidi wakes up from her nap, she'll remember she loves me, and then we will go away from you, terrible nasty goblin-creature."

"Pip, don't call Jeremy a goblin. That's terribly nasty of *you*. You need not stoop to his level." Chia slumped her shoulders. "Can we use the dust or not?"

"What is that?" said Jeremy, completely ignoring her question.

"Ouch, settle down, chap, you're making dents in my head jumping up and down like that," said Robert, still walking steadily along.

The sound of soft goat feet treading through the muddy field became muffled as Jeremy screamed in ohs and ahs of joy. "Did Clariel give you that feather? Tell me she did. Oh, please, please tell me it is what I think it is?"

His voice came toward Chia from the ground. She guessed he had fallen off Robert's head. She felt around for the feather on her lap. It's soft silkiness reminded her of the dress she had been wearing when she had arrived at 66 Lilly Pilly Lane. The dress that had belonged to Viola.

"Yes, she gave it to me, though she never said why."

Robert stopped unexpectedly, almost tumbling them all off his back. "This is marvelous news. Simply marvelous. We can travel anywhere with this feather. Clever Clariel. Clever, clever Clariel." Robert sounded delighted. And most happy to not have to walk anymore.

"Can I have it, Chia?" Jeremy's voice was right next to her left ear. And especially polite.

"Don't give it to him. I'll do it," said Pip.

Chia wanted to give it to Pip, but he had no hands to take it with. She didn't want to hurt his feelings. "I want nothing upsetting you. You need to focus on Heidi. Let Jeremy use the magic feather."

Pip snuggled into her arm. "You're a good friend. Yes, Heidi is all that matters. Give the fox the feather."

"Thank you! Thank you, thank you, thank you." Jeremy snatched it from Chia's hand and chanted in what sounded like gibberish.

Chia held in her stomach tightly. She squeezed both Pip and the sleeping Heidi to her even more tightly. She waited for the spinning feeling to start up, but nothing happened.

"It's not working." Jeremy huffed out in frustration and chanted a second time. "Nothing. We're still here. This makes little sense."

Robert cleared his throat. "Let Chia try. It is her feather. Maybe it only works for her."

Chia released her grip on the two ducks and reached out her hand. She felt the soft feather tickle her palm. What was this feather from? One of Clariel's angel wings, perhaps? "Do I have to chant like you did?"

"No, no, you daft girl," said Jeremy, his gruff voice nasty again. "Just think of the castle where Priscilla and Viola live. The one we went to. And think of all of us so we come with you. Of me and the goats and Heidi."

"And Pip," said Chia. She thought of them all, and couldn't stop her mind from wandering to Artemis and Ms. Roberta and even the house. For some strange reason, she thought of 66 Lilly Pilly Lane. It had always felt like a person to her. And everyone referred to it that way. She didn't mean to think of it. But how she longed to be back in its safety and warmth again.

A great gust of wind blew suddenly, as if a tornado was

near. It was so strong, it blew her onto the ground. She rolled herself into a ball, a sudden shrill sound penetrating her bones. An eerie, spine-tingling whistling noise filled the empty fields. What was happening?

Chia didn't know if it was good or bad or if she was the one who had made it happen with the feather. She clutched her feather tightly and hoped her friends were safe. She wanted to yell for them and find out if they were still with her. She wished she could see. What a gift her sight had been. In that moment of swirling wind and fumbling thoughts, she understood how much she had taken it for granted in the two days she had been able to see.

"Chia! It worked. You did it." Robert sounded tired and out of breath.

"Lucky break," came Jeremy's sarcasm.

"Your High—you also thought of my Roberta, didn't you?" Robert's voice was very high-pitched, even for him.

"Chia, you brought the whole house here," said Pip.

"Doesn't surprise me she couldn't get one bit of magic right. Predictable." Jeremy made a clicking noise with his mouth, as if to say, "You're too dumb to do anything right."

Chia ignored him. "Is Artemis here too?"

"Yes, he is, Your H—" Robert coughed again. "Still unable to move, I'm afraid."

"Where are we?" Chia stood up and dusted herself off, relieved she didn't have to travel for days on Robert's back.

"Lucky for us the magic brought us to the field outside

the castle and not inside it," replied Robert. "We all would never have fit inside, anyway."

"And everyone's safe? Pip, are you all right?"

"Yep. I'm fine."

"What do we do now?" said Chia. How would they get inside, find Pricilla, and defeat her?

"Don't move or we'll hurt you. You're coming with us."

Chia shuddered as she heard the voice. It was deep and gruff, and she recognized it immediately. Hitchens! The mine master. He had been so unkind to her. Half starved her, overworked her in the mines, and hit her for fun.

She stood up on her tiptoes, trying to seem taller than she was. She clutched the feather and thought of Hitchens turning into a frog. Or a rat. Or a fly. Or better still, she imagined him disappearing into thin air and never troubling her or anyone else ever again. She hoped her imagining had worked. But there had been no wind this time. No noises.

"Well, well. If it ain't Chia. I missed you down in the mines. Glad you're back to help find more diamonds. And even better you brought some friends along. They look like good workers."

"I order you to let us go!" said Jeremy. "I'm the general in charge here, and we'll be forced to attack if you don't surrender."

"A talking fox? You rotten little weasel. Did you steal diamonds from the mine when you ran off?'

"I never! I didn't steal anything." Chia's insides were about to explode.

"Liar!" Hitchens screamed behind her.

"I demand you let us go immediately, or I'll set all these goats on you," Robert threatened.

"Haha! I've over fifty of my men ready to attack you. And I would gladly add roast fox to my dinner. And roast goat. And those two juicy ducks look delicious." Hitchens had no fear in his voice. Only tones of winning.

"We surrender!" Chia tucked the feather into her jacket pocket. She put her hands up into the air.

"Chia! You can't just give up like that," said Jeremy.

Hitchens spat at the ground. "Hector, you stay here and guard the goats. I'll take Chia to see her dear mother, who's missed her terribly. Then it's back to the mines for you, Chia." Hitchens laughed, the sound whistling through his front teeth. His hand squeezed her arm so tightly her arm went numb. How Chia hated him!

"I won't come with you unless you let my two ducks and fox come with me. And the talking goat."

She felt something hard jab her in the back of the legs and fell to her knees. The pain seared through her legs, up her back, and to her neck.

"You're in no position to make demands. It's you and you alone. Take it or leave it. Otherwise, I'll kill them and bring them with us. Dead!"

"How dare you, you rascal! You heathen! You—"

Chia heard a loud whacking noise, and Jeremy stopped speaking suddenly.

"What happened? What did you do?"

"He assaulted Jeremy, that's what he did," said Robert, disgust in his voice.

"You're next," yelled Hitchens.

"Go, Chia," Robert encouraged her. "I'll tend to Jeremy. You can do this." Robert's voice soothed Chia's soul. She thought of her friends and her sister. She had to find her and rescue her. But she wasn't sure she could do it alone.

"Please. Go. For all of us." Robert's belief in her melted her fear away.

"I would come, but I need to look after Heidi," said Pip. "You can do it."

Chia wondered what she should do. But then the piercing pressure of Hitchens's hand around her arm reminded her she didn't have much choice in the matter. "I will come with you. Take me to Priscilla and Viola." She stood up, rubbing her sore back.

"That's exactly where I'm takin' ya."

Chia ignored his cruel laughter and his murmurs to himself. Her arm ached from Hitchens's pressure still pulling her along. She allowed herself to be dragged, dread dredging through her as she prepared to come face to face with Priscilla once more.

17

A DARING RESCUE

The pain in Chia's arm throbbed all the way into her fingertips. Hitchens pulled her along, no idea of the pain he was causing. Or perhaps he knew exactly how much pain he was causing and was enjoying hurting her. Chia wanted to spit on him. To yell at him. To hit at him.

She stopped, resisting his pull and holding her ground. This was the second time she had the urge to stand up to him. The first time was in the mines. What had come over her that day? It was like something inside her had snapped. That same thing was snapping in her now.

"Let me go, or I won't come with you." Her tone was as icy as Priscilla's and laced with indignation.

She took the one second of Hitchens loosening his grip to pull away. Her arm slipping from his hand, she walked backward, not sure what he would do. It was especially strange he had not yelled at her in response. Or slapped her.

"Come near me and I'll—I'll—" She remembered her

bow and arrows. She was still carrying them. No one had taken them from her. She reached for them, fumbling in her own darkness and fear of the silence.

But it wasn't silent for long. A long scream she was sure belonged to Hitchens made her skin crawl. And then several bangs, and a whooshing sound. A magical whooshing sound. She hoped it was Viola. Or someone come to save her. Someone that hated Hitchens as much as her.

"What's happening. Viola, is that you?"

But it was Pip's voice that responded. "You work for me now, Hitchens. You're *my* servant. You *love* to serve me. You'll do *anything* for me. Say sorry to Chia for hurting her. Confess to her you've been a stinking, nasty, beastly skunk. *Say it.*"

Hitchens whimpered. "I'm sorry I 'urt ya. I'm a stinkin' nasty beastly skunk, I am."

Chia froze in surprise and delight. Pip had escaped the soldiers and used his Mind Weaver on Hitchens. Chia breathed out all her tension. "You're NOT forgiven. Pip, how are you here? What happened?"

"We're all here," said Jeremy.

"I hit him with my Mind Weaver. This thing is so much fun. I can't wait to use it on someone else."

"Save it for Priscilla," said Jeremy. "And I still don't like you."

"Fine. I still don't like you either." Pip quacked loudly.

Chia heard lots of footsteps coming her way. She hoped it wasn't more soldiers trying to stop them.

"Here we are!" Robert's voice soothed her. He sounded like he had just won a war. "We beat them all. Every last one. Nasty soldiers. They're not even human. Robot soldiers. Can you imagine—she's using the diamonds to make soldiers! I tell you, it's criminal."

Chia heard the familiar sound of goats agreeing with him. "How did goats defeat soldiers?"

"Hit them between the eyes with a horn, and it deactivates them," said Robert.

"You are clever. And Heidi? Is she all right?"

"Yes. She's here safe and sound," said Pip. "She's extremely upset she can't talk. But once we get Clariel and the heart back, and she's back to her usual self, we'll plan our wedding. You'll be our bridesmaid."

Chia heard Jeremy grumble from beside her, "She hates you." Pip didn't answer him, and she hoped that meant he hadn't heard. There wasn't time for more squabbles.

"Pip, can you make Hitchens take us to Clariel and Viola?"

"Great idea. Horrible mean man, take us to Clariel and Viola. I command you." Pip sounded like he was an army general. And he was definitely enjoying the power from the way his pitch danced around the room.

"Clariel is in the dungeons," said Hitchens. "Viola is upstairs with Priscilla. Where do you want to go first?" He sounded a little robotic himself, since being hit with the Mind Weaver.

Chia was relieved to have the upper hand for a change. "Take us to Viola."

"No, no, no," Jeremy argued. "Don't listen to her. She's a child, what does she know? Take us to Clariel." He was being bossy.

"Pip, make him take us to Viola," insisted Chia.

"*Quack.* Sorry, Chia, but this time I have to agree with Foxy. Take us to Clariel."

"Why? Pip!" Chia was cross, but she knew the reason he had chosen Clariel over Viola. He had said more than a few times that he didn't like Viola. She wasn't sure why. Viola had only ever been nice to him. And to her. Yes, she had stolen the heart and Clariel but only because of Priscilla.

"Don't you dare argue on this one," said Jeremy. "With Clariel's magic, we can get Viola more easily."

"Fine. Lead the way."

She gave in, her nerves as sharp as a barbed-wire fence. She softened as Jeremy's soft paw wrapped around her ankle, showing her the way forward. There was his soft spot again. He didn't show it often. But when he did, he was especially kind. Still, she wished Artemis or Ms. Roberta were here with them. It twisted her heart into knots to know they were frozen solid and would not come back to life unless she succeeded.

They walked in silence for a few minutes. Chia ambled stiffly down the long flight of stairs, concentrating hard not to slip and fall. More soldiers attacked them. Lots more soldiers. They all approached from behind, but with over six thousand goats trailing along, overcoming the soldiers took no longer than a minute or two.

Chia pushed herself against the wall, several soldiers

brushing her as they went tumbling down the stairs. Banging and clanging noises filled the air. She hoped that Priscilla wouldn't hear the calamity. Her castle had been stormed, after all, and was being taken over.

But as they continued on toward the dungeons, no more soldiers came at them. The dungeons themselves seemed peculiarly unguarded.

A soft crying noise drifted into Chia's chest and sounded like the muffled cry of a child. "Someone else is down here too. Tell me what you see, Jeremy."

"Oh no," said a random goat.

"It can't be true," said another.

"We're doomed," said a third.

"What's happened? Is Clariel not here?" Chia continued walking toward the sobbing cries.

"It's Clariel," said Jeremy. "She's—she's—she's—"

"It's too much for me to bear!" cried Robert, breaking into tears too. All the other goats followed suit until the whole room trembled with sadness and sorrow.

Chia felt sad too. She wasn't sure why exactly. She didn't know what had happened to Clariel. She was an angel. What could Priscilla possibly have done to her? But this overwhelming feeling of guilt and grief was impossible to resist. She felt somehow responsible.

As the sobs came to a standstill, Clariel's voice was softer than a whisper. "Please don't look at me. Don't feel sorry for me. I can't bear it."

No one spoke. Chia knew she shouldn't, but she couldn't bear to not know. "Tell me what's happened." She said it ever so softly.

Clariel answered her. "I've lost all my color." She sobbed again, waves of depression palpable in the room.

Robert spoke with pride and courage. "You may have lost your color and magic, but you are still Clariel to us. You will always be the maker of the fairy dust."

Chia couldn't believe her ears. Fairy dust? How could an angel make fairy dust? Fairy dust wasn't real. Fairies weren't real.

"Huh? Please explain," she said, keen to find out more.

"I am, or was, a butterfly," said Clariel, now raising her voice.

"You still are a butterfly. Being white isn't so bad. It's better than being brown," said Jeremy.

"A butterfly?" Chia began to understanding that Jeremy had lied to her.

"Chia, I'm sorry I—"

"I don't care for anymore of your lies," she told him.

"I create all the fairy dust," Clariel said. "It was bad enough becoming small after the curse, but now this. I can't bear it. I can't go on." She burst into tumultuous tears that echoed off the walls and bounced off Chia's skin, making it crawl with lies and new information. The curse again. What *was* this curse?

Chia stamped her foot. "Fairy dust and curses! I'm sick and tired of not being told anything."

"We can't tell you," Robert said.

"How am I supposed to defeat Priscilla when I don't even know what's going on? You're unfair and mean, and —and—and—I don't know. I can't explain it. I feel mad and confused and bad. And you won't tell me what's going on. I don't want to be here anymore. You're all rotten liars, and I don't think any of you deserve my help. If it weren't for Viola, I would leave now. I would rather be back in the mines than here with you all."

She was surprised by what came out of her mouth. She hadn't meant to say that. She hadn't meant to be so mean, so unsure of herself, and so defiant. But her pride was bruised, and her mind was dizzy with disorder and darkness.

Clariel spoke up. "You're right. We should have told you everything from the beginning. We were being selfish. We were thinking only of ourselves. Of going home. Of being reunited with our loved ones. You're right. We used you. We should have told you everything. We want to tell you now. But we ache for home as much as you ache for your freedom. Without you, none of us can be saved. Without you, we're doomed for eternity. But we don't deserve to be set free. We will tell you everything, and so be it, if we remain trapped forever more. You see, you're—"

"Stop!" Chia surprised herself with the strength and speed of her call. Clariel's words had reached inside her chest and squeezed her heart tightly. Her friends wanted to be free too. If they were under a curse that only she could break, then break it she would. What difference did it make if she didn't know everything? Artemis had told her it was important she didn't know. She had to trust him now. She would help them. "I don't want to know. I don't need to know. All I want is to save Viola. Let's get out of here and get that heart back."

She spun in the direction she had come, sniffing her tears back, and wiping her eyes against her shoulder so no one could see her cry. Something deep in the recesses of her brain popped and stirred with some memory. Not a conscious solid memory. But a thought. Only she could save them.

This felt true and right and precious. She wasn't sure how she knew, but she did. She marched forward, hoping she wouldn't walk into a wall or trip over something.

"Bravo!" yelled many goats at once.

"I'm . . . proud . . . of you." Jeremy sounded like it was hard for the words to come out.

Chia smiled down at him, then looked over her shoulder and called, "Come on, Pip. You and Heidi will have a wedding yet. And Viola and I will be your brides-maids. Together."

Back through the cold, stark castle they marched. Back toward Priscilla. Back to fear.

"Where are we?" Chia asked.

"We're in the . . . oh no!" said Jeremy. "You try sticking me up your dress again, and I swear I'll bite you!"

"Prepare to lunge, my four-legged friends!" yelled Robert.

Chia stopped in place, crossing her arms across her chest. It had to be Viola they were talking to. Was she here to help them or stop them?

"Where did you get all the goats from?" said Viola, not sounding the least bit frightened or surprised to see them.

Chia was relieved and worried all at the same time. She wanted to run and hug Viola. But she also wanted to demand an explanation.

"I see you've rescued Clariel. Well played. Would you like me to take you to Priscilla?" Viola spoke slowly, carefully, and with no emotion.

"That depends. Are you on our side, or walking us into a trap, fair maiden?" said Robert. "Be careful how you answer. My goat friends have sharp horns that can rip you to shreds on my command."

His confidence impressed Chia, but she hoped he didn't mean what he said.

"I'm on your side. I got rid of the soldiers from the dungeons for you when I knew you were here so you could rescue Clariel. I've always been on your side," huffed Viola.

"*Humph!* You snatched me and stole all the magic. You turned me white. Don't trust her." Clariel's voice was etched with memories of pain.

"Chia, you trust me, right?" Viola said, ignoring Clariel.

Chia gulped down her doubt. "I think so. I mean, you did steal Clariel. Priscilla made you do that, right?"

"Yes. Yes, she did. I would never, ever, ever betray you," said Viola.

Chia stood in place, shocked. Ripples of electricity shot down her body. She needed to be sure Viola was good. To be absolutely positive Priscilla had made her steal Clariel.

"Chia, you don't belong with them. They don't care for you. Join me and we can run away right now—"

"Say one more word, and you will force me to—to—awoooo!" Jeremy howled like he was a wolf. "Pip, do it now!"

Chia guessed Pip would use the Mind Weaver on Viola. But that would only force her to say what they wanted to hear. This was her chance to find out for real. "Wait!" she called.

"Oh, this is silly, come on. Ignore these ignorant animals and come with me. I'm your sister. They're nothing to you."

Chia pulled an arrow from her back and flicked the bow into her hand. She concentrated with all her heart as she pulled back on the string, remembering her training. Training she had received from Artemis and Ms. Roberta. They couldn't help her, but their instructions echoed through Chia's mind as she pulled back on the string. She would finally do the right thing and find out the truth.

"Yes, yes! Do it," called Jeremy.

She let go of the string, thinking of her sister and of the truth. She was ready to hear it.

"You wretch! Ouch. That *hurt*. What's this, some cute little play set they gave you? Really, Chia, I thought—"

"Be quiet," Chia yelled. "Tell me the truth. Tell me why you took Clariel. Tell me that Priscilla made you do it. That she tricked you. Tell me you're good. That you've always been good. Tell me you mean it when you say you'll forget this place and all this magic and run away with me."

Viola gulped hard in reply. "Truth is . . ."

"Yes, go on, tell us," said Pip. "Fess up. It's truth time."

"I . . . hate . . . you. Always have, and you've forced me to do what I didn't want to. Soldiers!"

Chia's head turned left and right, not sure what was happening. She heard banging and clanging and yelling and yowling. A battle seemed to rage all around her.

But her heart was too busy splitting in two. She stood there frozen in place. Numb. Her sister had told her the truth, and it wasn't what she wanted, nor expected, to hear. "You hate me?"

"Watch out, Chia." It was Pip.

But Chia couldn't move. She didn't care to move. Whatever happened to her now, she deserved it. She had led her friends into a trap. She had led them here to save her sister, and her sister didn't want to be saved. She felt something hit her, then something else. She fell backward, not sure what was happening.

More yelling, but Chia didn't care to hear. Only Viola's words rang in her head. Words of hate.

But as Pip's words cut through the silence in her head, she forced herself to focus.

"My darling Heidi. What has she done?"

Chia sat up, feeling around with both hands. She felt a duck. Two ducks. Pip and Heidi. She lifted her hands up in the air, something thick and wet all over her hands. Pip was crying. "What's happened?"

More bashing and clashing noises, then quiet. "We beat them, but your sister has escaped." Robert sounded puffed out.

"Pip? Heidi? Where's Jeremy?" Chia felt around to the left and found the furry body of Jeremy. Limp and covered in wet, thick liquid.

"Your Highn—Viola has stabbed both Heidi and Jeremy," said Robert.

Pip cried so loudly it made Chia's heart thump with pain and compassion for him.

"Someone save her. Please!" he howled.

"Viola? She . . ." Chia sat in a heap, defeated and depressed. "Are they still alive?"

"Yes. Pip, you can save Jeremy. Quickly cry your tears into his mouth," said Robert.

"I need to save Heidi, not that horrid fox," said Pip, snorting back his tears like a pig.

"How? Why can Pip save him?" said Chia, lifting the fox off the ground and cradling his limp body to her chest. "I'm sorry, Jeremy. I didn't mean for this to happen to you. Quickly, Pip, help him."

"Heidi needs saving more than him," said Pip.

"Jeremy is dying. You must do it now, Mr. Pip," ordered Robert.

"*Aargh.* Fine!"

Chia felt Pip against her. She held Jeremy forward, her arms trembling.

"There, I did it. What about Heidi? Do I do the same for her?"

"No, she's fine. She can't die. She's immortal. She'll wake up in a moment," said Robert. "Well done, old chap, Jeremy is coming to."

"Oh, yuck, what's that disgusting taste in my mouth?" Jeremy had recovered.

"My tears! You just ate my tears! *Quack!*" Pip laughed and cried all at the same time.

"Your tears? Disgusting! That's it. This time I'm eating you for real. Ouch—why do my ribs hurt?"

Chia felt Jeremy collapse back into her lap. "You were stabbed. Pip saved you. With his tears, I think."

"We might have used a wee bit of magic on Pip earlier to make him talk again," said Robert. "It's still active. His tears gave Jeremy the magic he needed to heal."

"And Heidi? Are you sure she's all right?" said Pip.

"Quack quack!" said Heidi, coming to.

"Heidi, my angel, my darling sweet. You're alive." Pip sounded overjoyed.

"Oh, brother. That stupid duck was the one that saved me?" said Jeremy.

"Yes, he was. He gave his tears for your life," said Robert.

Jeremy gulped especially hard and loud. "I suppose, I'm kinda, what I mean to say is . . . Thwankou."

"What was that?" said Pip. "*Quack quack.* Say that again more loudly. I'm a little hard of hearing."

"I'm sorry I've been mean to you. There, happy?"

"And . . ."

"Thaaaank you," said Jeremy as if it ached him to speak.

"Hahaha! You're in my service for life, right?"

"Settle down, ducky! I won't eat you is all."

"Ever. As in never? And you'll never threaten me again?"

"Yeah, yeah, that. I won't eat you ever."

Chia felt Pip jump onto her lap and onto Jeremy.

"Mwah! Mwah!"

Jeremy wriggled away. "Save your disgusting kisses for Heidi. Revolting."

Chia's stomach grumbled. "I'm so relieved you're all

fine. And Pip, you're the bravest duck ever. I can't believe Viola did this!"

No one spoke. But Chia could sense the tension in the air.

"What aren't you telling me?"

"Viola was trying to stab *you*. Heidi and Jeremy saved your life," said Pip.

Chia shook her head from side to side. No. It wasn't true. It couldn't be. But the hard, cold truth surfed through her stomach and landed with a thump.

19

THE CHOICE

Chia picked up her bow and arrows and flung them onto her back. She was tired and especially hungry. Even stale bread from the mines would do. But she knew it wouldn't fill that empty feeling in the pit of her stomach. Nor would it take away her sadness. Viola didn't give much away when Chia had struck her with the magical arrow, other than to say she hated her.

"You're absolutely sure Viola tried to stab *me*? She wasn't aiming for Jeremy?" she asked.

"Nope. I was way over there," said Jeremy. "It was you she said she hated, you she flung herself at with her sharp knife. She looked like a starving wasp gone mad, and you're welcome I saved your life."

Chia stuck both her hands in her pockets. "How did Heidi recover on her own? Since when are ducks immortal?" She wanted to talk about anything else other than her sister. To think of anything else right now.

"Let's walk as we talk. I propose we head back to our camp, and try again in the morning," said Robert.

A whole chorus of goats agreed with him.

"Yes, I'm starving," said one.

"A good bit of grass and a nap will revive us," said another.

"Hear hear!" said the rest.

Jeremy growled. "What did I tell you about goats and their incessant need to eat grass."

"But we're here now, and Priscilla's room isn't far," said Chia. She wanted to get this over and done with. She didn't want to put off facing Priscilla for a moment longer.

"Your sister has escaped," said Robert. "And Hitchens with her. I'm sure they'll inform her we are on our way. It's very unlikely we will find her in her room. On the contrary, I think Priscilla may come and find *us*."

"Find *us*?" said Chia, cold whisking its way up her spine. "What will we do then? Now she has Clariel's magic, what does that mean exactly?"

"It means she can make more fairy dust. Powerful stuff, fairy dust. It can make practically anything happen," said Robert.

"Fairy dust or not, we'll be ready for her," said Jeremy.

Chia wasn't sure she believed in fairy dust, but she was scared of Priscilla, with or without her having any magic. Would she attack them? Would she hurt her friends? Was there any chance they could win? Even with so many goats, it seemed unlikely.

They walked back to the clearing in the forest where

Artemis, Ms. Roberta and the house stood, still and lonely. They agreed to hide Clariel high in Artemis's thick foliage. Even though she had no magic left, Priscilla may still want her back.

Jeremy curled up for a nap on the other side of 66 Lilly Pilly Lane, and Pip and Heidi went for a wander together. Chia wondered if Heidi wasn't secretly falling for Pip after all. She seemed to follow him about after his heroic attempt to save her. Robert and the other goats set about eating fresh grass.

Chia leaned her head on Artemis, glad to be alone with him for a while. She knew he couldn't talk back, but she felt somehow comforted by him. Maybe he could hear her despite not being able to speak.

"I'm sorry I let you down," she said.

She paused and imagined him talking back. "It's fine," he said in her mind. "You now know that your sister isn't all good. You'll make different choices next time."

"Yes, I will. I still find it hard to believe. It just makes little sense to me. She's only ever been good. I trusted her. But I will make it right. We'll all fight Priscilla and get the heart back, and then . . . well, I don't know what then. I suppose we'll bring you back to life, and live happily ever after. Without Viola." She stopped, her heart aching for her sister. She loved her so much. She had loved her father so much too. And now they were both gone. "Do you think there's a chance we can win against Priscilla, Artemis?"

"There is only one chance for you," shrieked a cold voice, hatred dripping from it like tar.

Chia jumped back from the tree. That wasn't Artemis's voice speaking. That was Priscilla. She put her hands out, unsure from what direction her voice had come. "Don't come any closer or I'll scream."

"No need for that, my dear. I'm here alone. I won't hurt you," said Priscilla, her voice purring like a tiger about to eat her.

Chia felt a cold hand envelope her wrist. "I won't hurt you, Chia. I'm here to offer you something."

Chia took a step back, pried her hand away, and pulled her feather from her pocket, pointing it forward as if it were a sword. She wouldn't hesitate to wish herself away if she had to. To wish all her friends away.

Priscilla laughed. "That won't help you, I'm afraid."

"It's magical. And if you touch me again, I will vanish. We all will."

"Full of surprises, aren't you, my dear? I must admit, I did underestimate you. I thought you were daft and weak and lacked the mental aptitude for anything in life. Still, I was kind enough to employ you in the mines, put a roof over your head, and give you food and water. I even let you keep that horrid duck."

"Employ me?" said Chia, using every bit of effort not to scream and lash out at Priscilla. "Hitchens hit me and fed me stale bread, and I don't remember ever getting paid to work. *Or* having a choice in the matter."

"*Pft*. There's no point reasoning with you. You're just like your mother, high and mighty and always thinking you're right."

Chia's stomach did a sidewards flip and landed upside

down. She felt her face grow hot. Her mouth went dry. "You didn't know my mother. She died when I was born."

"Well, your friends aren't very trustworthy if they haven't told you the truth." Priscilla took deep gulps as if air was a drink and she was guzzling it down. "I killed her. I took her heart. That heart you stole from me, that was her heart. And I sent Viola to pretend to help you take it back from me. I knew you were coming the whole time. I let you take it, *you fool*." She laughed like she had not a care in the world. She laughed like what she had done didn't matter.

Chia's knees shook. Was it because Priscilla had just told her she had killed her mother, or because her friends hadn't told her the truth, or because Viola had pretended to help her the whole time? She gulped down the new information, not sure what to say. She felt sick and weak.

"And now that I have Clariel's power, I'm unstoppable. Nothing and no one can stop me. I've created a perfect robotic butterfly able to make the diamonds into magic dust."

Chia lashed out with her arms, unable to hear anymore. But she found only empty air in front of her. "I won't let you. You're crazy and delirious and I'll find a way to stop you."

"You're blind, remember? You can't even see me. How will you find me without magic? I'm going to cast a new curse. A worse curse. One that can never be broken. One they will be stuck in forever. There will be no way to turn them back."

Chia stopped still, huffing and puffing. Her lungs

hurt, her heart ached, and her mind was defeated. Priscilla had won.

She was right. What could a blind girl do?

"Have you ever heard of Achilles?" said Priscilla, taunting her.

"What are you talking about? You've won, haven't you, so go. Leave!" Chia clenched her jaw.

Priscilla ignored her. Her voice was steely and raked with barbed wire. "Achilles had only one weakness. His ankles. It's how he was killed. You have a weakness too."

"I don't care what you think. Go away or I will call my friends."

"Your feet are the only part of you that aren't magical."

Chia didn't understand. She wasn't magical at all.

"I can kill you right now. Drive a stake through your feet, and you will die." She paused then spoke slowly. "But I won't . . . not yet."

"I've had enough of talking to you. You're a lunatic and I'm leaving." Chia squeezed the feather tightly in her hands, and thought of Lilly Pilly Lane. But just as she began to spin, her mind wandered to her feet. Her socks were the only part of her clothes that hadn't mended in the magical lake. And how her feet ached. They ached like they had walked across a dry, hot desert.

She couldn't leave. Not now. She thirsted to know more. Perhaps Priscilla was telling her the truth. She forced herself to think once more of the clearing outside the castle and of Artemis. Of Priscilla's castle. The spinning stopped.

"Why are my feet my weakness?"

"Good, Chia. Now you're speaking like a queen. A queen you will never have the privilege of being." Priscilla laughed like a hungry hyena.

Had she lost her mind? She must be lying. She had to be. But just as she was about to demand an explanation, a searing pain burst its way through the tops of both her feet, weaving its way to her soles. It felt like her feet were ablaze. She fell backwards, the pain unbearable.

"What . . . ahhh . . . what have you . . ."

"I changed my mind. You're a pest. I stabbed you in both your feet."

Chia reached forward, trying to stay awake, the natural urge to faint calling to her. She touched what felt like long sharp shards of glass, careful not to cut her hands. But no matter how hard she pulled, she couldn't remove them. Instead, they twisted violently, creating a pain equal to being trampled by one thousand goats.

A thin, wiry hand covered her mouth. Priscilla. Silencing her. A scathing voice spoke in her ear. "I will give you your life back. I can mend your feet, and you can live. All you have to do is agree to let your friends die in your place. All of them."

Chia wriggled to get free, but with the pain gliding its way up her legs, she felt the blood and life drain from her. She was dying. She could feel it. She let herself go limp.

Priscilla didn't loosen her hold over Chia's mouth. "I'll let you go free. You'll be free to live with your duck. A normal life, Chia. Give up your friends, and I'll let you live. Your life for theirs."

"Mmmm." Chia tried to say that she would never let

her friends die. Never. But she couldn't talk, her mouth still covered.

But Priscilla didn't let go. "I will even give you back your sight. You see, I can be especially generous. The alternative? You die right here. Right now."

She let go of Chia's mouth. Chia gobbled in air, trying to help her lungs keep fighting. To keep living.

"Your choice. Another minute or two and it will all be over. Your life and sight for your friends, or they live and you die. Save yourself."

Chia's couldn't feel her body anymore. She could hardly hear what Priscilla was saying. She could feel the last bit of life leaving her body. All she had to do was save herself. To put herself first. To choose to live. To choose to see.

But all she could think of were her friends: Artemis and Ms. Roberta. Pip and Heidi. Jeremy and Robert and all the goats. She couldn't let them die. She wouldn't choose herself over them. She would never do that.

"Chia! Last chance," called Priscilla, lifting her hand from Chia's mouth.

With what little strength she had left, Chia opened her dry mouth. "I choose to die. You'll . . . be . . . next."

20

THE MINES

Chia opened her eyes. She couldn't see a thing. She recognized the smell of dirt and damp air. She was back in the mines. And she wasn't dead. She was supposed to have died. What happened? The last thing she remembered was Priscilla yelling at her to choose her life over her friends'.

"Pip, are you here?"

Pip quacked loudly, calming her trembling nerves. "Please explain what I'm doing here?" he said. "Where is Heidi and the others? One minute I'm taking a nice night stroll with the love of my life and the next minute I'm here, in the stinky suffocating mines."

Chia cradled her head in her hands. She remembered. She remembered everything.

Everything.

Her mind flicked through a myriad of interlinked memories like photos in an album. Some images were black-and-white and faded, some brilliantly colorful, fresh, and new. But all of them fell into a perfect timeline. Her childhood. Her mother. She had memories with her mother and her father, together. All three of them. And she could see in her memories. She could see everything.

Where was Viola? No sooner did she ask in her mind than a memory of Viola being selfish and mean and unkind flashed before her. Brutally unkind. And especially selfish. She had never been good. And she was the blind one, not Chia!

Then a memory of Viola sprinkling her with something. And her forgetting. She had forgotten everything. And then she was in the mines. Her memories black now. Only darkness and the cruelty of Hitchens filling her head. And then a voice. A kind and gentle voice. The voice of hope and freedom. Ms. Roberta. Then Ms. Roberta whisking her away to 66 Lilly Pilly Lane. Her memories sped up now, like on a fast drive. She had gained her vision, and helped her friends to gain Priscilla's heart, and then lost it again. And then . . .

Chia stopped the movie in her mind and shook her head hard. The truth was too hard to bear. Her whole body shook uncontrollably as she remembered the words of Jeremy and Robert playing through her mind. She cried. And she yelled. There was no one but Pip to hear her.

She was the daughter of the queen. The daughter of the queen *of the fairies*. She was the only one who could lift the curse. Her friends had told her everything. She remembered. She remembered everything, and it burned a giant hole through her heart. They had sprinkled her with fairy dust and made her forget. Their one and only chance to save themselves and their kingdom. And Chia had failed. She had failed them. She had failed Viola, and she had failed herself. Again and again.

The only way to save them was to choose herself. To put herself first. To be self loving. To save herself.

She remembered everything, and it hurt throughout her body. She had set her friends free and gave her life in their place. But now she understood that Priscilla had tricked her. Priscilla knew that Chia would choose her friends over herself and now they would never be safe, nor would she. She cried harder than ever before, all her pent-up emotions flowing all over Pip as he hugged her tightly. She would never see her mother and father again. She had failed everyone.

"Don't cry. It's all right. We'll find a way out," said Pip.

"No. It's all over. I ruined everything. Artemis tried to tell me. Jeremy, too, but I didn't listen. They're all trapped forever because of me. And now I remember, but it's too late. If I know about the curse and how to break it, it can't be broken.

"Priscilla tricked me. She wanted me to choose my friends. She knew that if I did, they could never break the curse. I was supposed to pick to save myself. I understand that now." She sucked her tears back up her nose and squeezed her eyes shut. "Viola was bad all along, and I didn't listen to you or anyone else. I'm a fool."

She wished she could blink her eyes and go back to when she knew nothing. To when she was in the mines, oblivious to the truth. Oblivious to who she really was.

Oblivious to her sister's betrayal of her. But she couldn't. Her heart felt like it was being pinched between the fingers of a ferocious giant. Her breath was strained and short, and her feet hurt. Her feet really hurt.

She touched them, squirming as she pressed on the big dents on the tops and soles of both feet. Marks made by the glass Priscilla had stabbed into them. She pulled off what was left of her torn socks.

Her feet were the only part of her that weren't magical. Her feet had healed somehow, but the throbbing pain was a reminder she had a weakness. A weakness that Priscilla had known about and hadn't hesitated to use. Nor would she hesitate to use it in future to kill her if she didn't obey her.

"Snap out of it," said Pip, jumping up and down. "We need to come up with a plan."

"No, I'm done trying to save other people. I'm staying here and doing my job."

"Glad to hear it." It was Hitchens. "Ya rotten gutter poo. Get back ta work."

Chia heard Pip cry out in pain. Had Hitchens hurt him?

"Pip, are you all right?" she asked, feeling helpless without her vision.

"Quack. Yes. That ruffian kicked me. He kicked me."

"And I'll kick you again if I 'ave ta. Start diggin', you two. We need more diamonds. And I won't be putting up with ya nonsense again."

Slap! Slap!

Chia rubbed her cheeks, heat and tension moving

through her body. She wanted to strike back at him. But she didn't dare. She had lost. This much was clear.

"I ain't all bad. Haha." The laughter whistled through his teeth, grating Chia's nerves. "I got company for ya. Someone to be miserable with ya for the rest of ya worthless lives in the mines. Someone to help ya dig for diamonds."

Chia wondered who he was talking about. Was it Jeremy? Or Robert? She heard soft footsteps.

"Chia. Is that you, my darling?"

Chia felt arms envelope her. She knew instantly who this was. It was the strong embrace of her father. Priscilla hadn't killed him. Could it really be him? How she longed to look upon his face.

He kissed both her cheeks. "I can't believe it's you, thank goodness you're safe."

"What a touchin' reunion," mocked Hitchens. "Get to work, both of ya. I ain't 'ere to make dreams come true. That's your job. Diamonds for Priscilla. Get diggin' or I'll kill the duck, for real this time."

Pip ruffled up his feathers and waddled forward. "How dare you speak to me like I'm a common duck? I'm a talking duck, and I demand you tell me where Heidi is or else—"

Chia guessed Hitchens wouldn't hesitate to kick Pip again. She reached forward, risking being hurt herself. She found Pip and swept him up while holding his bill shut. "He won't be troubling you again, sir. None of us will. We're getting back to work."

Hitchens didn't speak. Chia imagined he was eyeing them like a lion, deciding which of them to eat first.

She heard his footsteps leaving the mines. "If I come back and ya haven't found at least ten diamonds each, there's no food for either of ya for a day. And you'll get a beatin' to boot."

Chia turned to her father. "You're alive. I'm so sorry I didn't look for you. I thought you were—"

"Dead, I know. My darling girl, how I've failed you. She had me hidden in the painting."

Chia flung herself into her father's arms, so relieved to have him. To hug him again. He was alive, and this more than soothed her aching heart. "That was you in the painting? The one I thought looked at me. You really were looking at me. Why would she set you free?"

"Priscilla is more evil than you can imagine. She would never set me free. It wasn't her. It was you. I'm sure of it. Your magic set me free."

Chia thought back to everything she had done from the moment she was rescued from the mines to now. She hadn't done anything magical at all. She had only made the wrong choices. "I don't think so, Father. I have done nothing right the whole time. I've been so wrong. I thought you were dead, and Viola was good, and all I could think of was to save her."

Chia felt her father's strong hands take hold of both her arms. "You're a good person to think of others. And it's to be admired, but—"

"I know, I know. I must put myself first. Artemis told me this . . . I didn't understand. How do you put yourself first when others are in need?" She breathed out hard, frustrated at her own failure and lack of insight.

Despite all she had done for everyone else, she had failed them, anyway. She had let them all down.

Her father let go of her. She heard him tapping at the mine wall with a pick.

"What are you doing?"

"Here, hold this," he said, handing her a diamond. It felt sharp and angular in her hand. "You're like this diamond. Bright and magical, but hidden in the dirt. To shine, you need to remember who you are. You need to find yourself. Not worry so much about everyone else. They'll find their own way."

Chia shook her head, not fully understanding. "But Priscilla puts herself first. She doesn't care about anyone else but herself. Viola too. That's what makes them mean and self-centered."

"Chia, putting yourself first doesn't mean not caring about other people. In fact, it's exactly the opposite. Viola and Priscilla go out of their way to hurt other people. If they truly loved and appreciated who they were, they wouldn't do that. You're worth it, Chia. You're next in line to be queen. And you're a fairy. If you had chosen yourself, if you had saved yourself, then you would be powerful now. Powerful enough to defeat Priscilla once and for all."

Chia gulped down the words her father was saying. She still didn't completely get it, but she knew he was right. He had always been right. She remembered how strong, loyal, confident, and brave he had been. And her mother too.

She had given up her place among the fairies to marry him. She had put herself first. She had put her own happiness before her people. Chia knew she was probably meant to do the same, but still she yearned for Viola and Artemis and Ms. Roberta and Jeremy and Robert and the other goats, to all be safe and well.

"It doesn't matter now, anyway. I've failed. It's all over, and Priscilla's making a curse they'll be trapped in forever." She felt around for a pick of her own. Finding it, she struck hard at the wall, wishing she could stop that horrible squeezing feeling in her chest.

"It's never too late to change," said her father.

"If I'm meant to look after me, then I need to stay here and not cause any more trouble. To stay safe. I have you and Pip. That's enough for me."

Pip waddled up to Chia and rubbed himself against her leg. "Is it really what you want, Chia? Is it really enough for you?"

Chia dropped the pick and shook her head. "What I really want is to show Priscilla that I'm better than her. I want to teach that brat Viola a lesson. I want to give Ms. Roberta, Artemis, Jeremy, and the others a fighting chance to save themselves." She closed her eyes, understanding for the first time her own words.

Her father was right. She needed to help them help themselves. Not do it *for* them. "And I want to see Mother as herself again. She's the most powerful fairy there is, isn't she?"

Her father took her face in his hands. "No, my darling. You are!"

21

THE WISH

Chia was back in the mines. Trapped once more. But this time she not only had Pip, she had her father, alive and well. This time she knew exactly who she was. She was a fairy. She was next in line to be queen of all the fairies.

"Do I have fairy powers?"

"Yes, my darling, you do," said her father.

"But my feet. They're my weakness?"

"Yes, that part is my fault, I think. It's the human part of you, like me. I always thought your feet were especially pretty."

"That's something. Nice feet that can kill me."

"But I managed to sneak these here with me. No one seemed to notice them. They were left in front of the painting I was stuck inside of."

Chia dropped the pickaxe and put out her hands, wondering what he was talking about. The rubber squeaking told her straight away what it was.

"The boots Ms. Roberta gave me. I wonder—did she

know when she gave them to me that I especially needed them?"

"Yes, I think she may have even put some magic in those shoes for you. No one noticed them, moved them, or took them from me."

Chia pulled them on, feeling more grounded and protected. Feeling like they had secret superpowers. She reached for her bow and arrows, only just realizing they were gone. She felt inside her pocket. Her feather was also gone.

"Yep, they took my Mind Weaver too," said Pip, sounding solemn.

Chia shuddered to think what Priscilla had done to her friends after their conversation. She doubted she had kept her word and set them free.

"Please tell me we can escape. I need to save Heidi," said Pip.

"A plan to escape? There's no way of getting out of here. Hitchens will catch us. There are bound to be guards all around the exit."

"There is another way out," said a soft echo from below. Chia gasped, positive it sounded like Clariel. Chia was sure of it. She looked down, sure the voice had come from her body somewhere.

"A friend of yours, Chia?" said her father.

"It sounds exactly like Clariel. She must have snuck into your pocket. Stand still so we can check," said Pip.

Chia stood perfectly still as her father checked her pockets.

"Yep, got her. Oh, a Dust Maker. What has happened to your colorful wings?" said her father.

"You're hurt," said Pip.

"Yes. I'm very weak," said Clariel. "I fell from right up high on Artemis into Chia's pocket just as she was being dragged away unconscious. I don't think I can last much longer. We butterflies don't live forever like fairies do. And I'm afraid my time is almost up."

Chia was mortified. Clariel was dying? "Father, we have to do something. We have to help her."

"No, Chia," said Clariel, her breath stunted and pained. "My time is done. But there is one last thing I can do to help you. To help you all."

"She might be our only chance," said Pip.

Chia nodded against her better judgment in agreement with Pip. She didn't want Clariel to use the last bit of her energy helping them. She needed to help herself.

She needed to help herself!

That was it. What Artemis was trying to tell her the whole time. And what her father had been trying to get her to understand.

"No, Clariel. You're not allowed to help us. Not one bit. The only person you need to help is yourself."

"Chia?" said Pip.

"Let's hear what she has to say," agreed her father.

"We each have to think of what we want. We each need to help ourselves. I understand now. Artemis was trying to tell me the whole time." She held up the diamond her father had dug out earlier. "Help me find more diamonds. Two more, I think, might work."

She scrambled for her pick and struck at the wall. Finding diamonds wasn't all that easy. But she seemed to have a knack of knowing where they were. Her father helped her, his one hand cradling Clariel. Pip pecked with his bill, eager to help too.

"Here's one," said Pip, triumphant.

"Well done, Pip. One more," said Chia.

"Got one," said her father.

Unable to see, she gave the orders she knew would work. She didn't know how she knew. She just did. Another hidden memory moving its way forward in her mind, perhaps. "Place all three diamonds on the ground, with the tips all touching, to create a circle, then put Clariel in the center."

Her father did as he was asked.

"Clariel, I want you to use your last bit of energy making fairy dust."

"I cannot. Priscilla took all my power," Clariel argued.

"No, she didn't. I'm sure. Your power isn't something anyone can take from you. It's who you really are. You need to do this for yourself. I want you to make this fairy dust for *you*. Not for anyone else. I want you to make this because you love to make fairy dust. Not to help me, not to help anyone. Make it because it's what you love to do!"

"I'm not sure I know how to do that." Clariel sounded exasperated.

"Please try. Please?"

"Yes, Your Highness," she responded.

Chia held her breath. This time, not because she was anxious. Not because she was worried. Nor because she was scared. This time she held her breath because she was hopeful. She crossed her fingers and prayed this would work. *This one's for you, Artemis.*

She listened for what might happen. At first nothing at all seemed to occur. Then a small but hopeful tinkling noise rose, like a tiny bell ringing. Slowly, the ringing got louder.

"Tell me what's happening."

"Clariel is making gold light," said Pip.

"Keep going, it's working," encouraged Chia.

"More gold light is jumping from diamond to diamond," said her father. "It's bleeding through each of the diamonds, turning them into gold dust. Oh my! It's extraordinary."

"What? What is it?" said Chia, tensing her shoulders and hoping it was only good.

"A beautiful kaleidoscope of color is curling its way across Clariel's wings. They're glowing pink and red and blue and green."

"Fantastic!" Pip sounded like he didn't believe what his eyes were seeing.

"Describe it. Please?" Chia had been right. It was working.

"The lights from Clariel's wings just turned one pile of dust to green, and the other purple. So cool," said Pip.

Chia felt a soft breeze flutter on her face. She sensed more magic happening. That and the fact that Pip was now yelling in quacks.

"You were right," said Clariel. "You did it. I have turned back to my normal self. I am so grateful."

Chia smiled from her face right down to her belly button. "You're colorful again?"

"Yes, that, but I'm also back to my right size. You remember the sheet I was hiding behind in the house?"

"Yes. It was very strange."

"It was because I had shrunk to the size of a regular, ordinary butterfly. I was ashamed. Embarrassed. But you've helped me to change myself back."

"You did that, not me," said Chia, relaxing for the first time in days.

"You're right. I did that." Clariel chuckled.

"What size are you, exactly?" asked Chia, noticing Clariel's voice seemed to come from up above her.

"She's big! Huge! I don't know how I feel about a giant butterfly," said Pip.

Clariel laughed. "It's your turn now. Open your hand. This fairy dust may be useful to you."

Chia opened her palm and shook her feet nervously inside her rain boots as she felt the soft, delicate fairy dust. "Father?"

"Yes?"

"Do you think Viola could ever be good? Truly find it inside of herself to change?"

"I think she can."

"Oh, brother. You won't use this dust to save Viola again, will you?" said Pip.

Chia smiled. She shook her head. She would think only of herself this time. Chia knew she had been tricked repeatedly, but something in her never stopped believing in her twin.

All her memories now returned. She recalled when her sister was about to sprinkle her with fairy dust to make her forget. To make her forget that Viola was stealing her sight. To make her forget that their father was still alive. To make her forget that Viola was mean and nasty and ruining their family. Just as Viola was about to sprinkle Chia with fairy dust, Chia had urged her to rethink her decision. Viola had hesitated then. She had stopped and thought about it. The look in her eyes told Chia she didn't really want to do it.

This made Chia happy. But most importantly, it made her believe that her sister might truly save herself one day. Chia understood it wasn't for her to save Viola anymore.

"Nope. I was just wishing her well in my mind. This one's for me."

Chia closed her eyes and sprinkled fairy dust all around her. What should she wish for? Freedom? Fun? To be far, far away from the mines? To save her mother? Her friends?

This wish had to be all about herself.

"I wish for my fairy wings. I wish for my true self to return!"

22

WINGS

Chia still had her eyes closed, the teensy weensiest bit of guilt creeping its way up her throat, but she swallowed it away. She wouldn't feel guilty about this one. Not one bit. Having wings and being a fairy was what she wanted, and she was glad to have made the perfect wish.

A bright spark of light erupted first behind her right eye, then behind her left. A stinging sensation drilled in the recess of her shoulder blades. And a fresh breeze fluttered across her face.

"Did it work?" she asked, afraid to open her eyes.

"You can look for yourself," said her father, clapping his hands together.

She opened her eyes slowly, like a bear waking from its winter snooze. One eye, then the other. She could see! Her eyesight had returned. She could see her father, and Pip, and Clariel. Clariel was as big as any person, flapping her colorful wings happily at her.

But something was flapping at her from behind too.

Chia looked over her shoulder and opened her eyes even wider. Could it be true? The most beautiful cherry-red wings with gold tips that were as long as she was tall flapped about her with a mind of their own. She held her breath and concentrated on them. She imagined them lifting her up. And they did. They lifted her up above the others. She really had wings.

"I'll be back," she called, thinking of nothing but herself for a change. She imagined zooming and zipping through the mines. And her wings followed her every command. She imagined flying faster, and she did. She flew through every part of the mines. She flew so fast, she passed Hitchens blocking the doorway and swished past the soldiers lined up outside. She was flying so fast they didn't notice her at all.

She was outside, free for the first time. She flew up into the sky, pausing as she got to an especially fluffy white cloud. She felt extreme exhilaration, not only from being up so high, but from the view below her. She could see everything.

Exhaling heavily she realized the mines were beside Priscilla's castle. The mines must have been right under Lavender Hill this whole time. Had her mother known this when she had picked this place to live? Was she guarding the mines the whole time? Guarding them from greedy humans like Priscilla?

She teared up a little, and her wings slowed their flapping. She descended slightly. This had been her home. She had loved it here. And now it was all destroyed. Dug up and destroyed. She wiped her face.

She needed to stay focused. She needed to keep her emotions in check. She needed to decide what to do next.

This time she wouldn't give up so easily. This time she wouldn't be selfless or selfish. There was a third option, she realized. Self-care. She had to do what was right for her. And she knew without any doubt she needed to leave this place forever. She needed to get away from here. Away from Priscilla. Away from Viola.

She closed her eyes and wondered what other sort of magic she possessed. She thought of her friends, Artemis, Ms. Roberta, Jeremy, Heidi, Robert, and the other goats. And she thought of her mother. Of 66 Lilly Pilly Lane. She had to at least know they were safe before she left.

She flew down to the large opening in the field where she had last seen her friends and hid in the tangled branches of a very large tree. At first she thought the tree must be Artemis, but as she followed the large trunk below her, there was no paper bark. And this tree was growing acorns. Voices from below beckoned her to keep quiet. She folded her wings back out of the way so as not to be heard or seen, and listened.

"I did nothing, I swear it," came Viola's voice from below.

"You little wretch. If you're lying, I will destroy you. Put you to work in the mines with your sister."

Chia shuddered at Priscilla's threat. The evil woman didn't care one bit for Viola. Yet Viola was obedient to her. Why?

"I promise you, Mother. I didn't disobey you again. I

did nothing magical to break the curse. Nothing. You have to believe me," Viola sobbed.

Chia leaned back onto the tree, her brain brimming with hope and happiness. Something had broken the curse. She knew deep inside it was her. She had done it. She had broken the curse. When she finally put herself first, she had not only gained her wings, she had set her friends free.

She climbed down the branches slowly and carefully so as not to make a sound. She needed a better look.

"Mmmm. Mmmmm."

Chia recognized the grunting disapproval of Jeremy. She peered down carefully through the branches. But instead of a fox, there was a goblin. She knew instantly it must be him.

Goblins weren't at all how she imagined them. Jeremy was short and chubby, not lean and agile, like when he was a fox. He was bright green and had big pointy ears and a giant pudgy nose to match. The part that matched his fox form was his hair. It was bright pink. The same hot pink he had proudly worn as a fox.

Next to him was a woman. Chia guessed straight away who she was. She was dressed in a sleek orange catsuit and had brown hair tied back in a long ponytail. And giant silver wings. She wasn't struggling like Jeremy to free herself. Instead, she sat calm and relaxed, despite being tied up and gagged. Her big green eyes twinkled with mystery. Pip wouldn't be too pleased that the love of his life was no longer a duck.

Beside them, a huge man with coffee-colored skin and

giant muscles rippling through his white clothes stared up into the branches. His bright twinkling eyes were definitely the eyes of Artemis. This was not at all how she thought elves looked. She smiled back, happy to see the real him for the first time.

Next to him, a woman sat daintily, in a beautiful gold dress. But instead of having a gold body, Ms. Roberta had the softest peach skin Chia had ever seen. Her pale pink lipstick matched her eyeshadow perfectly, and her long blonde hair was spread out all over her shoulders.

Chia had to cover her mouth to stop herself from calling out to them.

She leaned in more closely, seeing yet one more person tied up. She knew straight away who this was. She had her memories now to remind her that there was only one person whose kindness and love shone like this. A golden glow emanated from her like sunshine. Her mother. 66 Lilly Pilly Lane was once again Queen Lilly Pilly.

Chia quickly moved behind a thick branch as her mother unexpectedly looked right at her. Did she know she was there?

"What was that? Something moved in the tree," said Viola, peering into the branches.

"It's nothing. Focus, Viola. You're the princess now," lied Priscilla. "We'll use the fairy dust to imprison them in a new curse. Or better still, we'll turn them into dust. Yes, that's even better. Then we never have to worry about them again." Her laughter was all crooked and bent.

"Yes, yes, yes! Then we can go riding on my new leopards, right?"

Chia cringed as she heard a loud slap. It was louder than Hitchens's slaps. She didn't dare look in case someone saw her.

"I'm sorry, Mother. I know this is important. I won't let you down. I will get the dust. Which color?" Viola's voice trembled.

Viola had said Priscilla treated her well, but that wasn't the case at all. Viola was just as scared of the woman as Chia was.

"Bring me the green and red and black. Yes, bring me lots of black. I think it's best I turn them all into dust. Another curse can only be broken. It's much safer to obliterate them from existence." Priscilla laughed like a crazy, cursed madwoman.

Chia bit down on her bottom lip and dared a peek straight back at her mother. Their eyes locked. She tipped her head to one side. Thoughts pushed their way into her mind. Thoughts that were not her own.

"Chia, you are all that matters. You must leave. Forget the rest of us. Save yourself and start again. Take Robert and the other fairies and go far away from here. Leave us behind. You must."

Chia shook her head, breaking eye contact with her mother. She gulped down the instructions like poisonous pills. Leave. Yes, that's what she had planned. That was the right thing to do. The only way forward.

Her eyes closed now, Chia thought of the mines. Her father and Clariel. Pip. Her head ached from the confusion. Should she leave and save the rest of the fairies, or stay and help her friends be free? She had already made the wrong decision so many times before. She was meant to do what was best for *her*. But deep within, her heart yearned for her mother. And for Artemis, Ms. Roberta, Jeremy, Heidi, and even Viola to be free.

Chia couldn't let Priscilla get away with using black dust to turn them into nothing. She couldn't let that happen. She wouldn't.

The thought of flying into the sky filled her mind's eye. Her whole body trembled as she flew higher than the clouds this time. Her wings were spread out wide, but her shoulders were wilted. "Sorry, Mother. I have to do this. You need me, and I won't let you down."

Thinking only of the mines, Chia zoomed downward to rescue her father, Pip, and Clariel.

Then she would face Priscilla once and for all.

23

THE BATTLE

The air under her wings made Chia appreciate how much she'd missed out on not knowing she was a fairy.

Chia was determined to do whatever was required to help her friends the right way this time. She wouldn't hesitate to use her wings, her nails, and her temper to defeat Hitchens and his soldiers. She wasn't going back to the mines. Ever.

She faltered a little, her wings suddenly as nervous as the rest of her. There were too many soldiers down below guarding the mine. They must know she had escaped. She felt herself dropping, but quickly recovered herself as a sharp arrow came shooting her way.

She somersaulted in midair, sweeping down like a charging eagle, practically touching the tops of the soldiers' large metal hats. Hats to match their iron robot interiors. She whooshed up again faster than she thought possible, another six arrows narrowly missing her.

She flew up higher than the arrows could reach and

floated in midair, squinting to see what she was up against. Hundreds of soldiers held bows and arrows toward her, loaded and ready to shoot. It was impossible to get past them. There was no way she could avoid getting hit.

Apart from her feet, which were safely snuggled inside her red rain boots, she was impossible to kill. Even if she was struck, she would recover.

She twitched her nose thoughtfully, considering her plan more carefully. She recalled Heidi being stabbed by Viola. It had taken some time for her to recover. If an arrow hit her and she fell unconscious even for a short period, this would still give them enough time to catch her and tie her up. It wasn't a risk she was willing to take. She couldn't lose. Not this time.

Eyes closed, she waited for a new idea to arrive. It was still easier for her to think in the dark. An image of her own bow filled her mind. What a pity she didn't have it anymore. It would have come in handy. It wasn't deadly, but it would still have been a good diversion.

Chia plummeted toward the ground again, a new weight restricting one of her wings. She looked over her shoulder to see what was holding her back. There, sweetly nestled on her back, as if it had never been missing, was her bow and arrows.

She pulled them off, releasing her wing, and shouted with glee as she swished back into the air, twirling and howling like a wild animal. A very happy wild animal. Not only had she gotten her bow and arrows back, but she had just done magic. Magic she had created herself.

Did whatever she thought of come to her so easily?

She tried again. This time she thought of her feather. The one Clariel had given her.

Nothing happened.

She closed her eyes again, this time visualizing it more fully in her mind. She could see the red feather clearly.

A soft tickling sensation on her nose made her sneeze. She opened her eyes and saw the feather descending rapidly past her feet. She fell with ease toward it, caught it, and flew back up. Another sweep of arrows tried to hit her, but she was safely out of their reach.

She held the feather and smiled at it. It looked exactly like the feathers on her own wings, cherry-red with gold lining. She understood now why she was the only one who could use this. Clariel had given her one of her own fairy feathers.

Chia clutched it to her chest. Her magic was incredibly useful. She could travel places with ease and wish things to come to her. With this feather, she could get back inside the mines and rescue Pip, Clariel, and her father.

She could then collect Artemis, Jeremy, Ms. Roberta, and Heidi. And her mother. It was the perfect plan. It would be easy, fast, and nobody would get hurt.

She looked at the feather with new appreciation, readying herself to whizz and spin through the air and land in the mines. She tried to clear her mind, and think only of herself and the mines. But images of Robert, and Ms. Roberta, and Artemis crept in too. Her mind was doing its crazy thing again of thinking out of control. And then her mother popped into her mind, and Jeremy, and

Heidi. And all those sweet goats that could sing. They had been singing in fairy song the whole time when she first met them.

"*Aargh!* Stop thinking of everyone," she ordered herself. But then her mind flashed images of Priscilla and Viola too. "No!" she called, guessing what was about to happen.

But it was too late.

Her thoughts all stopped still, and the spinning started up. She turned as fast as the Earth spinning through space. She tucked her wings to her shoulders just as she landed face first in dirt.

She knew it had worked, but as she spat out the dirt of the mines, she looked around, mortified by what she had done. Not only was she in the mines, but everyone else she'd thought of was too. Including Priscilla.

Chia backed away, almost tripping over a goat, as Priscilla marched toward her, kicking goats out of her way. "How did I get here? Chia! It was you. You have wings." She sounded like a tornado about to destroy everything and everyone in its wake.

Chia stomped her foot into the dirt. Darn it, she had thought of Priscilla while still thinking of getting into the mines.

"I'll get her for ya," said a tall, fat man, scars ridged across both of his cheeks like a knife had cut him. She guessed straight away it was Hitchens.

He was climbing over goats, and the look of madness in his eyes told her it would not be good if he caught her. She tried to jump from goat to goat, but they were pushing all over the place, probably wondering how they were suddenly inside an enclosed space. And why they had not returned to their fairy selves. They were still goats.

But she had wings! She did. Chia lifted herself off the ground slowly, so as not to knock any innocent goats, and floated above their heads. She could see Jeremy, and Heidi, and Ms. Roberta, and Artemis too, all in their real forms and all tied up. And her mother. She was there. And her father and Pip were also tied up. Hitchens must have punished them when he found her missing.

"Your Majesty, you found your wings. Hoorah," sang Robert from below, waving his head at her happily.

"Hooray!" joined in a chorus of goats. Then they all started singing. Chia couldn't help smiling. She knew what the sound was now and allowed herself to float to the top of the caves. The goats, or fairies rather, all began to butt at Priscilla with their horns. She looked disheveled and confused. Chia was happy to see *her* suffer a little for a change.

Hitchens climbed the sides of the mines but with little luck on his side. Every time he got a little higher, a goat would bump him back down.

A scurry of mechanical soldiers descended on the goats. But each one was easily overcome by goat horns, hitting them one by one between the eyes, until there were no more soldiers left. Just a large pile of mechanical bodies.

Chia spread out her wings, preparing for her fastest flight yet. She would untie her friends at lightning speed. Deciding her bow and arrows would slow her down, she dropped them on the far side of the mines, far away from Hitchens. She could use magic to bring them back if needed. And where was her feather? She calmed her fluttering stomach, preparing to swoop down, but something stopped her. Something was holding her back. She flapped harder, but she couldn't move. She turned her head, heat rushing to her face.

It was Viola. Viola was holding her wings with a look of triumph stamped across her face. Her own large pink-and-orange wings flapped briskly behind her. She had wings too. She must have had them the whole time.

"Let go of me. There's still time for you to do the right thing. To be the sister I know you can be," said Chia.

"Huh! Be second to you? No, thank you, Your Majesty. I prefer Priscilla, thank you very much." Viola sounded so hoity-toity, like she always did. Spoiled and bratty.

Chia breathed out in frustration. "I saw Priscilla hurt you." Chia hoped to get through to her sister. "She doesn't love you. Mother and Father love you. They're down there, waiting for us to save them. They're our parents."

Viola scrunched her face, looking uglier than Hitchens. She gritted her teeth and tugged at Chia's wings so hard, Chia felt like passing out. But she didn't.

Instead, she kicked her sister, like a wild horse, as hard as she could in the shins. Chia felt her wings released and flew up slightly, glad to be free. She realized now that Viola wasn't going to listen to her. And Chia wouldn't be tricked by her a third time.

She prepared to fly forward when she heard Artemis call to her from below. She hesitated and looked down.

"Escape and leave us," Artemis yelled. Chia's friends were all being freed by the goats. She couldn't just leave them here. She wouldn't. What if Priscilla hurt them? She flapped her wings, planning to dive for them, but she was too slow.

In that one moment of hesitation, Viola had crept back up behind her and grabbed hold of her wings. A sharp pain moved its way through Chia's chest, down her back, and deep into her heart. A loud ripping noise echoed through the mines, silencing the singing below them. Chia felt herself falling. She fell faster and faster, luckily landing on soft goat wool. They had snuggled together to stop her fall.

She rolled onto the hard ground, shocked and in terrible pain. As Chia stood up, her legs barely holding her, the pain in her back now spread all the way to her toes. Her beautiful red-and-gold wings floated down after her. She felt like puking. Like crying. Like leaving. But instead she looked up at the smug, ugly face of her sister. "How could you?" yelled Chia.

Viola laughed, sounding more like Priscilla than Chia cared to admit. "No one said life is fair, sis." She flew above their heads.

"Well done, my dear." Priscilla, finally having moved away from the goats, accessed her fairy dust. She held blue dust in her palm and sprinkled it into the air, sending the goats flying into the wall. She pulled purple from her pocket next and blew it toward Chia's friends, tying them up again, and gagging them too.

And then she blew green dust toward Chia's beautiful wings, now lying on the dirty ground. They flew into the air, twirled like a pair of dainty ballerinas, and flew to Priscilla, fitting themselves perfectly onto her back.

"No. No! Give them back. They're my wings," cried Chia, but she was too scared to get them.

"Hahaha! You made it easier for me than I could have imagined. I have your mother's heart inside me once more, making me queen, and all I was missing was my wings. Well done, Chia. You came through again."

Chia fell to the ground. The pain in her body was easing now, but the pain in her heart was so strong she thought she might die of sadness. She had let everyone down. Again.

Priscilla blew gold dust toward Chia, raising her up into the air and freezing her in midair. Chia couldn't move anything except her head, no matter how hard she tried.

"Put me down. You've won. Let us go, please?" begged Chia, holding back a barrage of tears.

She could see, but right now she didn't want to. Her friends looked helpless. Only Jeremy and Pip were still fighting to be free. The others looked like they had given up. Even the goats were silent. They just looked stunned. And defeated.

"You've been a naughty fairy, Chia," said Priscilla, her voice as light and delicate as a fairy godmother's. "I don't think it's safe to keep you in my employ anymore. I think none of your lot will do. But how am I to find diamonds without you? You're so good at finding them for me. Well, they find *you,* in truth. But still. I'll have to replace you, I'm afraid."

"What are you talking about?" said Chia, trying to move, but still unable to.

Priscilla took another handful of dust from her pocket, this time black.

"Before I get rid of you, I want you to see your friends turn to dust. Yes, I can't wait for you to see how spectacularly you failed. I want to see your expression as I turn them to ash. They'll be gone forever. No more curses for them."

"Really, Mother? Would you? That sounds a little harsh," said Viola, showing the type of kindness Chia had been defending her for the whole time.

"Be quiet, you stupid girl. You'll have your turn."

Chia watched as Viola's face turned red. But instead of fighting back, she bowed toward Priscilla and kept quiet, hovering up at the cave ceiling.

"Viola," Chia yelled. "You have to do something. You met Ms. Roberta. She was kind to you. And Jeremy, and Pip. And Artemis gave you bark. Please?"

"Shut up." Viola crossed her arms and turned her back.

"Poor sisters. Twins too. What a shame you shall be separated. Much safer to have you two apart. Haha. Are you ready, Chia? Ready to see them all vaporize?"

Chia shut her eyes. She couldn't look. She wouldn't. But her heart ached for her father and mother. Her best friend, Pip. And all her other friends. She had to see them all, one last time. To tell them she was sorry. She opened her eyes, trying hard to move and fight. To do something. Anything. But she couldn't move. No matter how hard she imagined it, her magic seemed not to work against Priscilla's dust. She visualized her feather. But still nothing happened. Her mind was too scattered.

Chia felt a jolt of light and color burst into the caves, knocking Priscilla to the ground. It was Clariel. Chia hadn't even noticed that Clariel was missing. She must have escaped. Her voice shaking, she called out to her. "Quickly, Clariel, use your dust to stop her."

Clariel nodded her head toward Chia and dived for Priscilla, a look of intense focus on her face. But Priscilla, still standing on the ground, was ready for her. As Clariel descended upon her, blowing pink dust toward her, Priscilla was prepared. Her black dust rose into the air prepared for Clariel's fairy dust.

Chia winced, holding her breath, and counted to subdue her anxiety. She watched, acutely alert, as the pink and black dust met in the air, playfully dancing around each other. The black dust looked like a cat trying to catch a pink bird.

As the pink dust pushed its way past the black dust and toward Priscilla, her face turned green at what was about to hit her. But the black dust rose into the giant form of a tiger, and flew faster and faster. Seconds before the pink dust hit Priscilla in the face, the black dust devoured it in one gruesome gulp.

Chia let out all the air she had been holding. What would happen next?

Clariel flung orange dust, and yellow and red and purple into the air, all of them meeting together like a rainbow wave. She looked pleased with herself and clapped like a child. The rainbow headed toward the black dust with eagerness. The black dust morphed into the shape of a volcano and bubbled blackness toward the rainbow, collapsing it into nothingness. The blackness paused, then moved without hesitation toward Clariel. She covered her head and folded her wings, aware of what was coming for her.

"No!" yelled Chia. This couldn't be happening. Someone had to do something. "Help her," she called toward Viola, who was watching with a look of horror on her face. "Save her."

As the black dust hit Clariel, she coughed uncontrollably, and then piece by piece, each colorful part of her body, her wings, and finally her head turned into nothing more than dust and vanished.

Chia sobbed. Her heart felt numb. Her mind confused. "You can't do this. There's no fairy dust without her."

"Poor Clariel. She's had a terrible lot of luck since you lost her. What's happened to her is all your fault, Chia." Priscilla stood back up and reached into her pocket, pulling out more black dust. "Time to say goodbye to your friends now."

Chia looked down at them all, and cleared her throat, speaking as loudly and bravely as she could. "I'm so, so sorry I failed you. Please forgive me."

Priscilla was right. She had caused everything. All of

this was happening because of her. Tears gushed from her as she looked into the eyes of the goats. They were terrified.

Jeremy, Pip, Ms. Roberta, and Heidi all looked so overwhelmed by fear. She had never seen such looks of despair before. Her heart ached for them. She couldn't believe this was about to happen. Not like this. Not because of her.

She looked at her father, his eyes smiling back at her. She had thought he was dead all this time, and here he was. She had only just gotten him back, and she was about to lose him again. Last of all, she looked at her mother. What splendid secrets 66 Lilly Pilly Lane had kept, but none as good as the fact that the house had been her own mother the whole time. And a fairy queen at that.

I'm so sorry we can't be together, thought Chia. She was about to see them all turned to dust. She had lost. Their lives were all about to end.

24

BLACK DUST

Chia's mind, defeated and empty, sat there as limp and lifeless as the rest of her. There was nothing she could do. She was powerless. *Help me think of something, please Mother.*

Her mother's reply rang in her head, every word crisp and clear and contradictory in her mind. *"My special one. You have the power to change this. You are the most powerful fairy there is. All you have to do is save yourself. Think of yourself first. Put yourself first. And everything else will be fine."*

I don't understand. Artemis had said this to her so many times. She had tried, and still it hadn't worked. She looked into Artemis's eyes for some clue of what she could do. Nothing was working. She wasn't strong enough. She couldn't fight Priscilla and win, no matter how much she put herself first. Artemis winked at her, then closed his eyes.

"Farewell, putrid fairies. You won't be missed. Haha," howled Priscilla.

Chia watched in slow motion as Priscilla put the black powder to her lips and prepared to blow her friends and family into oblivion.

Her mind raced faster than her wings had. Her mother had just said she could still do something. If she only thought of herself. But she didn't know how to do that. Every time she was meant to have saved herself, she had gone back to her old ways.

The only way to save them was to think of her feather and get them all out of here. It could work if she concentrated hard enough, despite Priscilla's black fairy dust. She had to try. Chia closed her eyes and thought of her red feather, her mind filled with self doubt.

But as the rancid sound of fairy dust floated through the air, and the sickening magic hurled all around her, she knew she was too late. She opened her eyes, no feather anywhere about, and watched in horror as the black dust moved its way past all the goats and turned them into dust. Then Artemis, Ms. Roberta, Heidi, Jeremy, her mother and father. Gone. They were all gone like rainbows blown away by a thunderstorm. Chia felt frozen in a nightmare, unable to escape as Pip, last of all, her best friend in all the world, melted away into nothingness.

"Nooooooo!" Chia finally found her voice. "Please turn them back, please? I'll do anything you want. Please turn them back. This can't be real. This can't be happening. Do something." She felt her insides go cold and hard. Her desperation to save them turned into sorrow. Tears streaked down her face, dripping onto the ashen dust. The remains of her friends.

The room was empty, except for Hitchens, Viola, Priscilla, and her.

"Kill me too. I don't want to live. I can't live in a world with all of them gone. Do it," cried Chia.

"Poor Chia. Everyone's dead. And all because of you," taunted Priscilla. "You tried to break the curse and you failed. You tried to save your friends. And you failed. Haha. You're *pathetic*."

"I am, I am pathetic. Kill me, please. I can't bear the pain."

"All in good time. First, we need something of yours. Come here." Priscilla blew yellow dust at her. Chia felt her limp, lifeless body move toward Priscilla.

"Let me kill 'er, missus. She's been a right old brat, she has. Let me do it." Hitchens walked toward Chia and spat in her face, the spit rolling off her cheek.

She had lost everything, and everyone. She didn't care what he thought of her. She had nothing left to lose. She only had herself now. She was the only one left.

Chia looked Priscilla in the eyes and wished with all her might that she'd drop dead on the spot. "You're ugly. My wings look awful on you. You don't deserve them."

"Haha. If I cared what you thought, I would have asked you. In any case, you'll be dead in another minute."

Chia yelled in agony, unable to move, as Priscilla stuck her hand into her chest. She grimaced as she saw her own plastic-looking heart in Priscilla's hand. A true fairy heart, she now understood.

"Is that the only way you can kill me? Because you know I'm now the rightful queen. Is it?" said Chia, the force of anger she had so successfully pushed down now raging to be set free. "You'll never be like me. You'll never be any match for a *real* fairy. You can pretend you're one, but you're nothing but trash from the gutter. You're nothing and no one."

Priscilla grimaced at her words, then cleared her throat. "I was going to give you a kind death like I did the others, but on second thought, I might let Viola's leopards eat you. Now shut your mouth."

Chia bit down on her trembling lip. "What will you do with my heart?"

"Oh, don't worry my dear, I'll let you see before you die. It will please me to see you suffer even more." Priscilla blew powder into Chia's face, moving her back up into the air. Chia watched as Priscilla took out another fairy heart. Someone else's. She put it to her lips. "Come here, Viola."

Viola, who had been flapping about on the ceiling of the mines the whole time without saying a word, flew down as if she were being commanded.

"I want you to kill Hitchens. I've no need for him anymore. Kill him. That's an order!"

"You're joking, right, missus? I've been nothing but loyal to ya." Hitchens turned to run.

Viola opened her palm to receive some black dust and blew it toward Hitchens without hesitation. "Please, lady, have a heart," he called out, running. But the black dust was too fast for him.

Chia looked away as Hitchens's body disappeared like the others. She shouldn't feel sorry for him after all he'd done to her, but she did. No one deserved that.

Priscilla smiled like a shark. "Come here, Viola."

Viola flew to Priscilla's side.

"She's so well trained, don't you think, Chia? You did not save your sister after all. She was selfish and mean when I met her. But still not bad enough for me. I used fairy dust on her from the start. It was her heart I took first. And she's been doing everything I've told her to do since. I created a nastier, more selfish version of Viola. *A better version.*"

Chia couldn't believe her eyes or ears.

"She took your eyesight because I told her to. When you were in the tunnels, she really tried to help you. Willful little thing working against me. But once I found out, I set things straight. I got back control of her. She's my little pet. My daughter." She paused and pressed both the red beating hearts to her cheeks. "But alas, I've tired of her. She's becoming harder and harder to control. She'll be your replacement in the mines."

Priscilla lifted Viola's heart to her mouth, kissed it, then closed her fist around it, squeezing the life out of it. Viola bent over in pain.

"Viola!" But it was too late. Again. This time Viola's heart crumbled into red dust, and Viola fell to the floor, unconscious.

"You killed her? You're a monster!"

"Haha. Some have called me worse. Don't worry. I have the perfect replacement heart. One you won't need anymore." Priscilla leaned over and stuck Chia's heart into Viola's chest. Viola instantly came to life. She sat up and rubbed her eyes. "Mother?"

"Yes, child, I'm here," said Priscilla, rubbing Viola's arm like she was sweet and kind. And sincere.

"I can't see. Where am I, and what was I doing?"

"You're in the mines where you live hunting for diamonds. Off you go. Find me lots and lots, there's a good pet."

"Yes, Mother," said Viola. She felt about for a pick. Finding it, she smiled sweetly, stood up and began obediently digging for diamonds.

Chia flared her nostrils, a guttural roar coming to her lips. She screamed as loud as she could muster. Priscilla had turned Viola into the monster she was. She wasn't all bad. She really had tried to help Chia when they met in the tunnels.

Priscilla was controlling her all this time, making her do as she ordered her to. And now Viola's heart was gone forever. Chia's heart was the only thing keeping her alive.

"Your turn, petal. Time to join your friends in nowhere land."

Chia had to do something. She had to save her sister. She was all she had left. She closed her eyes, not thinking of anything. Instead, she held the empty space, waiting to see what would come to her. An image of one of her red arrows appeared. She could see it in her mind as clear as a sunshiny day. It whizzed its way toward her.

She felt something strike her chest, just as she saw in her mind. A giddy, bubbly feeling moved through her whole body. It was as if she'd been turned upside down and inside out.

She opened her eyes and stared down to see one of her arrows had truly hit her. A gold light emanated from her chest, and the arrow was floating right beside her.

Chia looked up, seeing the look of joy on Priscilla's face as she blew the last of the black dust toward Chia. It drifted toward her, about to obliterate her, just like the others. This was it. She was about to no longer exist.

"Truth is . . ." Chia said, not sure where her words were coming from. "Truth is, I never liked you, Priscilla, when you came to work for us. Truth is, I wished you'd never come. Truth is, I wish you weren't ever born." She could feel she was yelling, but she couldn't stop.

"Truth is, I wish my mother and father still lived on Lavender Hill, in a house just like 66 Lilly Pilly Lane. Truth is, I want to be a fairy and grow up knowing I'm one. I want to fly with my wings and be free. Truth is, I want Viola to be nice and to see and to love me.

"And I want my friends alive as their true selves. Well, I'd like them to be as I first met them too. I want Pip, and Jeremy, Heidi, Artemis, Ms. Roberta, Robert, and all the other goats to be alive and well, and happy and free."

She gulped hard, a magical tingling sensation spreading through her whole body and pouring out of her mouth. "Truth is, I want you to turn into dust on the spot, Priscilla, and for none of this to ever have happened.

And most of all, the truth is, I WANT THIS ALL FOR ME.

"I want this because it will make me very, very happy. I am worth it. I deserve to be happy." Chia ran out of breath, or she would have kept talking. Her own magic arrows had struck her, and finally, she had told the truth. She had finally thought only of herself. She had finally said what she really wanted.

One minute Priscilla was smiling at her, looking rather amused. The next moment, the black dust she had blown toward Chia did a complete turn and headed right at her. Chia watched without a drop of pity as Priscilla's black dust hit her right in the face. She cracked like porcelain.

Chia fell to the ground and landed on both her feet.

Priscilla was falling apart, turning into dust.

Chia calmed her beating heart, took off one of her red rain boots, and kicked Priscilla right in the shins. She wanted the human part of herself to do it. She wasn't sure why. It just felt right. As her foot connected with Priscilla's leg, Priscilla's high-pitched scream was loud enough to crack her entire glass castle.

She made one last grab for Chia, but she was too slow. Like something out of a horror movie, Priscilla's face turned into dust, then her body, and finally her legs. She was gone. Even Chia's wings had turned to dust with her.

The only thing left on the ground was her mother's ticking fairy heart. The heart everyone had so desperately wanted. She picked it up and tucked it into her pocket. Then she pulled her red rain boot back on and turned to her sister, who was still tapping away at the mine walls, oblivious to anything happening around her.

"Viola?"

"Yes?"

The wind suddenly picked up. "We have to go," yelled Chia. It had begun softly but was now like a windstorm. She took hold of Viola's hand, no resistance in it, and squeezed it tightly.

Viola's eyes teared up. "I'm sorry I stole your eyesight and was so mean to you. I was a horrid sister, I truly was. I love you. I'll be better. I promise I will."

Chia's eyes teared up. All she'd ever wanted was to hear those words from her sister.

"I love you too." Chia hugged her sister tightly as she spun again. Only this time, the spinning was different. It wasn't like the time when Ms. Roberta had come to get her. Or like when she had used her feather.

This time she was spinning in a push-pull type fashion, like her whole body was being torn apart. She was spinning out of control. No matter how hard she tried to hold onto Viola, she couldn't.

She let go, a tunnel of bright white light opening up in the ceiling of the mines. Chia watched Viola tumble up into it. Was this the end? Were they dying too?

Chia closed her eyes, a soft warm feeling enveloping her. Her body felt electrical and magical. She was the most powerful fairy of them all. She trusted that whatever was happening was meant to. It was a good thing.

This wasn't the end for her and Viola. This was a new

beginning. She could see the bright light through her eyelids as she, too, tumbled into the light tunnel.

Chia thought only of all the people she loved. She smiled to herself. She'd won this time. She had killed Priscilla.

And finally saved her sister Viola.

25

HOME

Chia could hear birds chirping. A soft breeze caressed her cheeks, and the smell of chocolate chip cookies weaved its way up her nose.

Something tickled her face. She swatted it away. But there it was again. A curious stirring sensation between her shoulder blades made her sit up. She curled her hands around fresh blades of grass, her eyes still blissfully closed.

"Chia! Chia! Hurry up, we're about to have tea."

Chia craned her head forward in surprise. That sounded just like Viola. She opened her eyes, wondering where she was exactly.

She smiled at the lavender flowers and popping hues of purples gently swaying all around her. She was on Lavender Hill. The last time she had been here, Priscilla's glass castle had sat perched atop it, and the ghastly mines right below.

It wasn't here anymore. But nor was the sweet cottage

she had grown up in. Instead, standing before her tall and proud was 66 Lilly Pilly Lane.

She jumped to her feet, noticing her red rain boots still snuggly cradling her feet. She was wearing the original white dress Ms. Roberta had stolen from Viola. Except now it had a lovely red sash to match her shoes. She itched at her back, and almost fell over with shock. Her red and gold-lined wings had returned, and they looked and felt bigger and better than her original ones. This was what had been tickling her.

Chia's heart skipped a beat as a new horrid thought slipped into her head, like a nightmare, unwelcome and impossible to stop. What if she was in a new curse? What if her mother was the house again? She ran forward, climbing the steps two at a time, forgetting momentarily she could fly. She pushed open the front door, but hesitated.

"Are you going to stand there all day, Princess? Come in before the house changes its mind." It was unmistakably the deep, obnoxious voice of Jeremy. He was here too! But his tone didn't sound nasty, like normal. It was warm and inviting.

Chia stuck her head through the door, not sure what she would see.

Jeremy sat perched atop a toadstool, licking his bright pink fur, a knife and fork in each of his matching pink paws. "Hurry up, I'm hungry, and my roast duck is getting delivered any minute now." He smiled at Chia.

"You're dead, aren't you? I saw it happen."

"Dead? Why would I be here if I was dead? Come sit with me."

Chia rubbed her arms and shook her head. "If you're not dead, then I'm in a new curse. A curse worse than the last one. I mean, you're nice," she said, accidentally speaking the last sentence out loud rather than in her head. She'd always thought Jeremy being mean was hard to handle, but him being so nice was definitely worse.

Jeremy clanged his knife and fork together, laughing. "Curse? What are you talking about?" Jeremy's laughter turned into a choking fit. "You're acting very strange. *Hm.* I must get Robert to check on that . . . after my tea. I'm starving. Viola? Artemis? Hurry. Where's my duck? Chop! Chop!"

Chia, finally feeling her feet again, took a step through the front door. She looked around at the Haven Room. The house must still be her mother, she reasoned. She had to be. The curse couldn't possibly be broken. Everything was just as it had been before. And Jeremy was still a fox, instead of his goblin self.

"Where is Pip? If you ate him, I swear I'll shake you so hard—"

"Chia! Why would I eat Pip? We're best friends. What a mean and horrible thing for you to say." Jeremy frowned his big bushy eyebrows at her.

Chia felt dizzy. She sat down on a soft tuft of moss to get her bearings and squeezed her mind, trying to remember her last memory. But all that came to mind was all her friends being turned into dust by Priscilla. And then Priscilla turning into dust, and finally, she and Viola rising into that lovely bright light.

Chia blinked rapidly, taking in the Haven Room as if for the first time. It was even more dazzling than before. The sparkling lake and waterfall splashed on the ceiling, and there was now an upside-down rainbow. And a red slide joined the wonderful yellow tube slide that zoomed its way around the expansive room. But there was no giant tree in the middle. No Artemis.

As if on cue, Artemis walked through the mirror. But he wasn't a tree anymore. He was back in his elf body.

"Finally! What was keeping you so long? I'm hungry enough to eat grass," said Jeremy.

"Grass? Did anyone say grass? I'd love some, thank you," said Robert, following behind Artemis, and still in the form of a goat.

Chia was more confused than ever. Why was Jeremy still a fox and Robert still a goat, whereas Artemis was back to his natural form as an elf? It made little sense.

"If this is a terrible dream, I insist I wake up." Chia rubbed her eyes.

"A dream? Who's having a dream?" Viola skipped through the mirror next.

Viola was skipping? Viola never skipped, and she looked happy. Her face was soft and her lips rosy. She was wearing a plain purple dress and looked unlike herself. She skidded to a stop in front of Chia, offering a plate of chocolate chip cookies.

"Cookie? I baked them myself. Cool, right?" Viola waved her long ponytail around and danced on the spot.

"You look surprised, or sunburnt, or something. Were you in the sun too long again?"

Chia took a step back from her. "Is this real?"

Viola came nose to nose with her. She placed her cookies on the toadstool and leaned in to Chia's ear, her eyebrows lifted in glee. "You beat Priscilla. Don't you remember?" She picked up her plate of cookies and skipped to a nearby tree stump without dropping a single cookie. "Mother's bringing the tea."

But Chia couldn't move. She couldn't take a single step. Even her wings dangled, unsure, on her back. Viola seemed to know exactly what had happened, so why didn't she?

Ms. Roberta came through the mirror next in fairy form. She wore a green plaid dress and matching green high heels. And she had bright golden wings that matched her hair.

"Were you daydreaming outside again, Chia?" she called from across the garden.

Chia needed to ask Viola what was happening here, but before she had the chance, Artemis leaned down toward her. "Do me the honor, would you? Viola and Jeremy baked cookies and brewed tea and roasted duck, but I would rather fancy some pudding and pie for afternoon tea today. What about you?" As he finished speaking, his big brown face morphed into wood. His arms grew, long and spindly, into giant branches, and he grew taller and taller and taller, turning back into the tree Chia had always known him as. His big blue eyes sparkled at her.

"It is rather special having two forms, don't you agree? Now take some of my bark and wish me up a lemon meringue pie, thank you, and some rhubarb pudding."

But before Chia could do as she was asked, a little duck peeked its face around Artemis's trunk.

"Hey, Chia, have you seen Heidi? She said she'd come for a walk with me."

Chia snapped out of her trance, dropped the bark, and picked up Pip. "Pip, you're here too. I'm so happy to see you."

Pip nuzzled his head into Chia's armpit, then lifted it right back out. "I'm pleased to see you too, but we talked about this. I have a girlfriend now remember?" Pip jumped back down and waddled toward Jeremy. "Hey, pal, want to play chasey in the garden later."

"Sure, buddy old friend. Can I be a goblin or do I have to stay a fox?"

"Your choice today."

Jeremy hugged Pip to him like they were old friends.

Chia stood there in utter shock. Pip had a girlfriend and was best friends with Jeremy? Everything was topsy-turvy and back to front.

The mirror shimmered, and a ravishing fairy stepped out from it. She wore a tight orange jumpsuit, and her silver wings reflected light in all directions. It was Heidi in her fairy form.

"There's my gal. Later, dude." Pip gave Jeremy a high five with his wing and half walked, half flew to Heidi.

Heidi caught Pip like he was a football flying through the air. She cuddled him to her, kissing him on the bill.

Chia watched, exasperated, as Pip stuck his head in Heidi's armpit, his fluffy bottom sticking up in the air.

"Did he use the Mind Weaver on her again?"

"Mind Weaver? Why would he do that? Robert! Chia needs you. She's acting really weird," yelled Jeremy.

"Are you all right? You look unusually pale," said Artemis, transforming back into his elf body. He picked up the bark Chia had pulled from his tree form and conjured up his pie and pudding. And strawberries with cream too. "Maybe some afternoon tea would help."

Chia didn't feel like eating. Everything and everyone around her was wonderful. But she still couldn't believe it was real.

Robert cleared his throat. "May I have your attention, everyone? Yes, thank you, that's better. I'm afraid Chia isn't quite herself and needs some time to rest. We'll be back in a moment. Start afternoon tea without us." He turned to Chia and whispered, "Jump on, Princess."

Chia climbed onto Robert's back, feeling silly this time. The last time she had done this, she had no shoes and needed to ride Robert to get through the muddy patch. But she did as she was told.

"Feel better!" waved Ms. Roberta.

"See ya, Chia," said Pip.

"Goodbye," waved Heidi as she morphed back into her duck self and waddled away with Pip. Chia was delighted for Pip. He was truly happy, and that made her happy.

"I'm coming with you," said Viola, flying above Chia's head.

Chia nodded. She felt dazed. Joyful. But dazed. She needed an explanation, or she thought she might faint.

She passed through the mirror on Robert's back, into the long corridor. Was she going to see Clariel?

As she passed through the other mirror, she found herself in a new room she had never seen before. It was a large white room, scattered with colorful furniture. It felt happy and familiar. The blue couch and red cushions looked familiar.

She noticed her father's wooden rocking chair. And the quaint kitchen in the corner. This looked exactly like the house she had grown up in on Lavender Hill. It was all squeezed into one room.

"Your Majesty, Chia's here," called Robert. "She's arrived, but her memories seem to be delayed."

Chia bounced up onto her toes, relieved to see her mother and father. They were both dressed in everyday clothes. But her mother had the most splendid pink-and-golden wings. And a crown of the exact same colors on her head.

Chia threw herself into her mother's arms. Nothing in the past few days felt more real. She was home.

26

A NEW BEGINNING

Chia didn't want to let go. Not ever. Just in case everyone vanished again. She allowed her father's warm embrace to join her mother's, and Viola's face nuzzle up against hers. They were together again. And this time, they were happy.

"Oh, Mother, tell me this is real and not another curse."

"Yes, dear, of course it's real. Just as real as you and I are." Lilly Pilly released her arms and beckoned Chia to the couch.

"You all turned into dust, and then Viola spilled into light and then . . ." They wouldn't believe her would they?

Her mother smiled, reassuring Chia everything was fine. "I know dear one. Viola told me all about it. She only just arrived back yesterday."

"So we haven't been here?" Chia tried to make sense of it all, but she was struggling.

"You were here the whole time," said her father. "But

the you from the old reality just got here now. It's hard to explain. You changed everything. The old you has just landed back in this moment, with all your old memories and none of your new ones."

"We can't be sure why," said her mother, "But I think it's just a side effect of everything you did."

They were right. None of it really made any sense at all, but then not much did in this magical world. "But I can't remember anything from this reality. Jeremy and Pip are friends. Pip can still talk and Heidi loves him. And we're all living in 66 Lilly Pilly Lane?"

"Yes, we are. It's all thanks to you. You did it. You didn't just break the curse, you gave us all new lives," said Robert, nuzzling up against her leg.

"I did?"

"And you saved my life," said Viola. "Look." She reached inside her own chest, like it was a common everyday thing to do, and pulled out half a heart. "You have the other half. Now we're connected forever."

Chia's mother smiled and reached out a hand for each of her daughters. "I have both my girls back, better than ever. Chia, if you'll permit me, I will restore all your memories."

Chia craned her neck forward, feeling it go hot. "But I'll forget what really happened, and only remember this new life, right?"

"No. You'll remember all of it. The others don't know. We thought it best not to tell them. It would only confuse them. They have only ever lived this life. The life you created for them when that arrow hit you. Oh, my darling, you finally discovered what it meant to put yourself first."

Chia shook her head. "That's all I had to do the whole time? Just say what I wished I wanted to happen?"

"Not exactly. It was more than that. You had to speak your truth. To speak from your heart. This is hard for most people to understand. They think there are two options in life—be selfless or be selfish.

"I was the selfish one," said Viola.

"And I was the selfless one," said Chia, partly understanding and partly not.

"Yes, exactly," said their father.

"But there is a third option. And you needed to find it yourself," said her mother.

"I remember, when the arrow struck me, it forced me to think about what I wanted. What would make me happy. I didn't think those words, I just kind of felt them." She paused thinking back to how at the time she was free and fearless, despite black dust coming her way. "I wanted you all to be happy, but most of all, I wanted myself to be the happiest of all. I've never felt like that before."

"You're incredible. You saved us. You saved us all," said Robert, mewing happily.

"But why are you still a goat? And Artemis can be both? And Heidi, she changed too."

"That was you," said Viola, jumping up and down on the couch. "You said you wanted to live on Lavender Hill and for everyone to be here too, in their normal forms, but also in their other forms. Because you liked them both. Well, everyone can now be both. They don't know any different. I guess fairies are now kinda shapeshifters, sorta."

"And yes," said her mother as if reading her thoughts. "You have the power to make things happen with your mind. And to bring things to you. That's your gift. But it has to be for you. It won't work if you want it for any other reason."

Chia stood up and walked around the room, slowly taking in this new power of hers. She could make things happen. That sounded dangerous. What if she misused her gift, or made everyone vanish again?

"We'll help you tame your power. It will be fine. I promise," said her mother.

Chia looked into her soft brown eyes, so grateful for her. New air filled her with hope. "I'm ready for my memories now."

Chia's mother held out her hand filled with gold dust. The last time someone blew gold dust at her, it was Priscilla.

"Wait," called Chia. "Priscilla?"

"She doesn't exist. She was never born, just as you wished it to be."

"And Clariel?" she asked.

"She's safe in the mines, guarded by a herd of goats, happily making fairy dust with the diamonds."

"One more thing," she asked, unable to curb her curiosity.

"Chia! Will you let Mother give you back your memories?" said Viola, laughing.

"Sorry. I'm just wondering. Where is the fairy kingdom? And the other goats?"

"The other goats, I mean fairies, are at Faren. Grass is fairies' new favorite food," joked Robert. "Faren's the fairy kingdom where we all come from. You'll get to go soon enough. Once your memories are restored and you're made queen, you'll come back with me."

Chia stared at Robert, a mixture of butterflies and rocks wiggling around in her stomach. She was going to be queen? And go to Faren, the fairy kingdom?

"Last thing, I promise," she said.

Everyone laughed.

"Go on. What's another few minutes of forgetting everything else," said her mother.

"What do you look like, Robert? As a fairy, I mean?"

"I could just as easily show you afterward, but to appease your curiosity, my lady." Robert waved his arms about and twirled round and round like a carousel, white light pouring from him. When it dimmed, there stood before her a tall, lean, yet muscular man with a tuft of yellow hair and a matching goatee. Big white teeth smiled back at her.

"Thank you for saving me. Thank you for believing in me. Thank you all!"

Robert hugged her tightly. "It's Uncle Robert to you, actually. But you'll know that soon enough if you'll only let my sister, your mother, Lilly Pilly, finally sprinkle you with fairy dust," said Robert.

Chia jerked her head back and dropped her mouth open. Robert and Roberta were her aunt and uncle? She felt giddy all over. She had been protected and guided the whole time. She smiled, her heart filling up with sparkles of love and light. "I'm ready. I'm ready to remember."

She closed her eyes, a soft feeling of dewdrops in the morning falling all over her. Her mind flipped with pictures. Colorful pictures. New memories that felt like old memories etching their way over the black-and-white images in her mind.

She had grown up a fairy. She and Viola were the best of friends. They could both see. She saw Robert, her uncle, and Ms. Roberta, her aunt. She saw Artemis, sometimes an elf and sometimes a tree. She saw Heidi and Pip, who fell in love on their own. And Jeremy, a goblin prince, who gave his life for hers so many times. She saw it all.

There was no more Priscilla. There was no curse and never had been. They were all safe and happy, living on Lavender Hill.

But then she saw something that surprised her. Something she didn't expect. She saw a fairy. He stood at the end of her bed, night after night, and beckoned her. He was nothing more than a black silhouette. She couldn't make out any details about him, except that his wings hung limp. He was injured. Badly injured. She was sure. She concentrated hard, trying to hear what he was saying to her.

"Faren will die unless you save it." She was sure that was what the fairy said.

She opened her eyes sharply. "I have to go to Faren. It's in danger. I have to save it."

"Oh, brother. There goes everything you learned. All about you, remember?" Viola nudged her.

"What's this about, Chia?" asked her mother, concern etched across her forehead.

Chia looked at them all, a fresh appreciation for her new memories, yet pleased to have the learning from her old memories still intact.

A feeling drifted through her body. A knowing. Trouble was heading for Faren, and it was up to her to change it. She swallowed heavily, not sure how she would convince them, but she had to try. "It's my destiny to save it," was all she said.

A NOTE FROM THE AUTHOR
ELENA PAIGE

Thank you for reading The Splendid Secrets of 66 Lilly Pilly Lane. The idea for this story came to me one day when I walked past a giant house in my suburb. It looked like it belonged in a fairy-tale rather than a modern day neighborhood.

The truth is I didn't know at the time, or even after I started writing that my story would involve fairies! Or Goblins. Or Elves. But I did know straight away there had to be a tree as a main character. And a duck! I had the best fun ever writing the scenes between Pip and Jeremy. I hope you enjoyed them just as much.

My other inspiration for writing this story was the need to educate and teach people to put themselves first. Chia had to learn this the hard way. I want kids to live in a world where everyone is more loving and compassionate and I know this begins with how you treat yourself. Self-respect and self-love are the basis of kind and compassionate people. I've not read any other stories with a theme such as this and I hope it helps create a better world.

But this isn't the end of Chia's journey. Look out for the next book in the series coming in 2020… The Magical Marvels of 88 Enchanted Lane.

It would be awesome if you left a review or rating from where you bought the book. This helps other people discover the book. Thank you again for joining me on this journey. Until we meet again,

Stay magical!

Elena Paige

EXPLORE OTHER BOOKS BY ELENA PAIGE

TEEN BOOKS For children aged 9+ and for adults who love reading exciting fast-paced edge-of-your-seat fiction...

THE MAGICIANS SERIES:

The Magicians' Convention (Book 1)

The Greatest Magician (Prequel)

The Magicians' Academy (Book 2)

The Magicians' Battle (Book 3)

THE FAREN CHRONICLES:

The Splendid Secrets of 66 Lilly Pilly Lane (Book 1)

The Magical Marvels of 88 Enchanted Way (Book 2)

CHAPTER BOOK SERIES for kids ages 7-11...

EVIE EVERYDAY WITCH:

Secret Magic (Book 1)

Spooky Magic (Book 2)

Special Magic (Book 3)

For children aged 4-9…

TAKI & TOULA TIME TRAVELERS (early reader books):

Hercules Finds His Courage

Athena Finds Her Confidence

Zeus Tames His Temper

Hades Learns To Be Fair

Aphrodite Finds Her Inner Beauty

MEDITATION ADVENTURES FOR KIDS:

Lolli and the Lollipop

Lolli and the Thank You Tree

Lolli and the Talking Books

Lolli and the Meditating Snail

Lolli and the Bunyip

Lolli and the Magical Kitchen

Lolli and the Superfood Quest

Meditation Adventures for Kids - The Entire Lolli Collection

HAPPY HEART RHYMES (picture books):

I Love Being Free

I Love Being Different

I Love Trying New Things

ELENA PAIGE

loves creating stories which inspire and transform young readers. She writes from the heart and especially loves weaving magic into her books.

Her greatest value in life is *creativity* - nurturing it, enhancing it and using it. She loves inspiring children to believe in themselves and accept their own way of creating, even if it's outside the box. The most amazing creatives on the planet, rarely fitted in!

As a child, she thought magic was real and used to try convincing her teddy to come to life. Tired of waiting she adopted a Moodle dog, Lucky, that rarely leaves her side.

On Sunday mornings you can find her hiding under her Doona cover reading, while her children are wondering where their favorite book has disappeared.

Find her at www.ElenaPaige.com

facebook.com/elenapaigebooks

instagram.com/elenapaigebooks

pinterest.com/elenapaigebooks

Made in the USA
San Bernardino, CA
25 May 2020